STAINED-GLASS WORLD

Stained-Glass World

KENNETH BULMER

NEW ENGLISH LIBRARY
TIMES MIRROR

FOR PAMELA

First published in Great Britain by MacDonald & Co. Ltd. in 1969
© Kenneth Bulmer, 1969

*

FIRST NEL PAPERBACK EDITION JULY 1976

*

*NEL Books are published by
New English Library Limited from Barnard's Inn, Holborn, London, E.C.1.
Made and printed in Great Britain by Hunt Barnard Printing Ltd., Aylesbury, Bucks.*

45002763 5

1

He knew his way around the Twentieth Century; but at what precise instant of time complete and detached from the mill-run of common time itself he first placed his naked foot into the muddied water, brown as paint, in the gutter on the other side of the road, he afterwards recollected only dimly, luridly in patches, shot through with the zig-zag red-greens of mocking pseudo-memory.

He could feel the water, cold and absorbing, around his ankles. He could feel the night wind, sharp and toothy, biting into his skin beneath the cheap cotton pyjamas. Blue lights pea-podded the concrete road with vague illumination. Blown papers scuttled. Soon the rain would drive in with tongued lashes to drench but not clean this tawdry town.

A minute or two ago – he thought – he had been settling down comfortably on a couch in Guztav Lawlor's Luxury Relax Palace to take a trip.

He had decided, this time around, to call himself Wendell. An idea capered at the back of his preoccupied mind that he had gone down into the lower end of the city to find something out. A crisis had been threatening, a crisis, the gravity of which Sturm had failed to notice, was menacing the whole city. He was concerned only with his own city. Other cities in the world grappled with their own worries. One city contained enough of a man's life to illustrate the way of the world.

He took his feet out of the water and at once they seemed to swell, to contract with a loud crash, and then to warm up like mittened toast. He rubbed his hands together, feeling the bony knuckles smooth, like miniature skulls, and looked about him.

Where was he?

In the cold, that tiny part of his mind that never really let him be, said tartly. Take all this as real. Accept it as though it really existed. In face of the cold discomfort now bewildering him – a discomfort as chilling as the strictures of the Moral Aid cranks – he must find shelter and reorientation.

He stumbled back across the street, headed for the neon-lit bar with flapping doors. Darkness shrouded the pavement. A swooping isolation engulfed his spirits. He had no clear idea what was going on, or why. Acceptance of a pseudo-reality could not negate the coldness of the water, the scorching wind wickedly razoring his ribs.

Wendell was a tough enough man of his middle age group battling to keep fit with badminton and squash, light-handed with liquor, nor addicted to ordinary tobacco, taking his kicks in a jolt of Joy-Juice, and his body could absorb a reasonably high dosage of this kind of punishment. But he just did not relish the idea of wandering the cold and wet streets of a barren hicktown in the middle of the night. Particularly not when clad only in thin cotton pyjamas. Not even for kicks.

He hitched the trousers up and the cord broke.

Bending over and beginning a comprehensive anatomical curse, he glanced up, his eyes drawn by a new light source, and he did not bother to finish the curse.

Half bent over as he was, one fist gripping the waist of the pyjama trousers, the other fumbling at the flapping end of the broken cord, his face jutted out on a level with the apparition.

Central in a sickle-shaped opening into nothingness, hanging chest high in the night, the head gibbered and mewed and mauled, beckoning with wide grimaces, with rolling eyes, with suggestive nose-wrinklings. Wendell stared motionlessly at the apparition.

This was his kind of trip?

He would want this – a glowing Arab moon-shaped hole into insanity?

He would conjure this – a head that simpered and mewled and leered, urging him to join it in unknown, nameless sins?

Well, possibly. Yes, possibly, Wendell conceded, grasping his pyjamas and slipslopping across the road into the shadows beneath the building where the bar glowed like an illuminated cave of promised debauchery. He couldn't rule it out.

'Come back!' The head called after him, writhing its purple

6

lips. 'Come back, my lumpkin! You doanow what I c'n ofrit yuh! C'mon back, ninnynonkins!'

Wendell had no idea – no unearthly idea, no subconscious idea – what the thing could be. But subconsciously it existed as real as the ground beneath his slipperless feet.

The rain chose that blustery moment of choking insecurity to sweep its first broom-bristle swishings across the town, flinging water clamouring from tin roofs and echoing guttering, spouting from broken pipes, boiling white into the brown water of the gutters. Wendell hunched futilely into the sodden pyjamas and splashed like a ghost through the rain mists and silver bouncing bubbles of the rain.

They weren't even his own night attire.

He hopped agilely up on to the far sidewalk, straddling the swelling current. Old cans, orange skins, scraps of paper, obscene artifacts, chips of packing cases, all floating in that murky miniature Nile. He had to get out of the rain *muy pronto*; but the combination of thin cotton and water had made of the pyjamas a nudey show and, here in the twentieth century, if that was where he was, haven had become that much more difficult to find.

The moment had long gone when he could no more pretend he was enjoying all this. As an experience it had been great and salutary; but now he must be pushing along. He tried for a transition, expecting the emerald and brown interpenetrating squares to come pulsing down; but nothing happened. The wind dashed a spray of muddy water into his face. He looked at the bar, fuming.

The sign, half obliterated by rain, shone out ruddily.

LEAN   EDS

CH AP   RAT S HO W TER

With the rain dripping from his face Wendell looked up, squinting his eyes. What the hell . . . ?

Then he saw the unlit bulbs.

Clean Beds. Cheap Rates. Hot Water.

Oh.

He shouldered the door open, still clasping his sundered cord. If he had to he would invent some way of payment later. He was in no mood to argue. If this was one kind of reality he'd be hurled back into the gutter . . . This just *couldn't* be his own trip!

His apprehensions receded a little when he saw that the receptionist, alone and aloof in a glass cage, was a uniformed orang-outang. It smirked at him, wiping its wide rubbery lips, pouting.

'Yes, sir – a nasty night. Come in, come in. Put your bags down. The dromedary will take good care of those. Yes, sir.'

'I don't have any bags,' Wendell began.

'Just leave them right there. We understand.'

They'd not so far, Wendell thought, achieved this degree of humanisation of an orang-outang. They'd tried, of course, as they had tried all kinds of other animalistic tricks in the effort to create a planetary partner for homo sapiens. So that more or less reinforced this experience as a normal hallucination.

The light gleamed green and golden from the glass reception area, receding quietly from the vague tenebrous shadows beyond, creating the quietness and dust-tasting mausoleum-effect of small hotels. He would not go into the bar just yet. He could feel the cheap cracked linoleum beneath his feet, could hear the water drip-dropping from the sodden pyjamas, could taste the flat sourness in his mouth.

A woman with a half-masked angel's face and eyes like wasps glided from the shadows, her bejewelled midnight-blue gown aflame with coruscations, smiled obliquely at him, mounted the rickety stairs. She carried her leopard's tail in one bejewelled gloved hand. The black and yellow fur glowed against the half-concealing dress.

At once Wendell felt more at ease. Cat-women were familiar phenomena to him. Her smile had no power – now – to itch down his back, to make him flinch back with canine obstinacy.

'Room Twelve A, sir.' The orang-outang rubbered out the words glueily. 'You'll find it very comfortable.'

'You'll find it very – comfortable.' The Leopard-woman giggled, over-scarlet lips pouting around the words.

'Thank you.' Wendell felt this to be a normal trip hallucic now. He had been badly shaken. His annoyance over the uncontrolled existence of the hallucination clashed with relief that at last events were falling into an understandable pattern.

He allowed himself to wonder if this place could ever have been real. In time? In space? He didn't really know and he

8

doubted if anyone at all would ever know. Not that it mattered. Time and space were concepts far too big and outside his domain. He dealt with more subtle areas of life. Now he would cheerfully allow himself to be carried along by the illusion.

He walked towards the stairs.

'Your bags, sir.' The orang-outang smiled with toothy deprecation. He looked like an incredibly evil old man.

An hallucinatory bite from those sharp teeth could take an hallucinatory mouthful of his flesh and shed quantities of hallucinatory blood and give him an abominable hallucinatory pain.

'Thanks.' He went back and bent down without looking to where he would have put his bags if he had had any, and his fingers struck polished plastic handles. Resignedly he hefted the two zip bags, feeling their weight and seeing with a comical quality of detachment the many airline and hotel stickers mottling their red rexine plastic. Not his bags. He wouldn't trust himself in reality to an aeroplane.

He felt too weary to say tartly: 'Give the dromedary a tip for his services, will you?'

The stairs creaked a fiddle obbligato as he ascended.

A rapid oscillating pattern of indigo, emerald, ochre and ivory impacted squares flashed like a descending and enveloping curtain before his eyes. His foot struck a riser instead of landing on a tread. He bent forward with his hands grasping the cases like straws. His trousers stayed halfway up his legs, tacked glueily to his flesh. He blinked. The multi-chequered pattern blipped and vanished.

An interesting transition at last. . . .

There was no transition.

'I'm waiting, Bung.' The voice below him spoke with a touch of acerbity like bitten bitterness.

Wendell looked down hastily, nearly overtoppling. The man waiting below, wearing a leather jacket and carrying two cases identical to those carried by Wendell, tapped a leather-booted foot impatiently on the stair. Dust puffed.

Nothing could be as it seemed. Caution turned Wendell about and sent him climbing the stairs.

'Twelve A!' shouted the orang-outang insultingly.

'I'll have to rest up a bit. Then I'll attend to this confounded hallucic.' Wendell pushed the imitation mahogany door open and blundered a pace into the room. A sour smell of unventilated places slicked unpleasantly on his tongue and he made a face. The darkness closed down with a denseness stifling reason. A uterine fog possessed him. He dropped the cases and stretched out his hands, feeling like an infant along the wall, seeking the round reassurance of the light switch.

At his touch light sprang out.

He stood on a single bare plank, his back pressed against the wall, staring out on nothingness. No room. No bed. No walls. No ceiling. With the light came wind. Wind that scorched at his tissue-thin pyjamas with a thousand scalpel edges. Below his naked feet the gulf waited blackly, its hollow darkness riddled with millions of flecked crimson flames, the watchfires of the unappeased dead.

Around him the air rang with laughter, the terminal laughter of the surreal pushed beyond the brink of despair.

A scattering of hammocks in the Mary Roberts Ward already hung empty, each like an abandoned nylon chrysalis, still swinging blankly. From most of the hammocks arms and legs projected uncaringly. The air held a flat dead taste of lavender. The whole area of the ward had been utilised to swing hammocks, a hundred and fifty feet by ninety under the vaulting pre-stressed ceiling, and Conrad had either to duck under or squeeze past in a manner displeasing to him in its affront to his own ideas of propriety.

Not that the trippers would feel anything if he jabbed an angry toecap into a rounded bulge as he passed. But the principle of the the thing obscurely annoyed him, particularly as he well knew there was ample room in the other abandoned wards of the disused hospital.

He did not like the sleazy feeling of the hammocks against his dark green shirt and slacks. His shuffling footfalls sounded a deadened note against the floor as though he wore wax earplugs. Outside in the sunshine on the concrete ramps his footsteps had rung loud and crisply.

There seemed no way of relating the people in the hammocks to the capabilities, for the ambiguous labour codes on the ident labels at each hammock head would inevitably be smudged. Conrad flicked peevishly at two or three, trying to

10

unscramble the wavering illegibilities of men and women too far gone in anticipatory debauch to bother over writing a clear hand – those that could still bother to write, this was. Many – too many, Conrad felt with impatience – compromised their indifference to the world with a thumbprint.

Tony Lawrence shouted across the hammock-packed ward, his voice bouncing unexpectedly in the acoustic maelstrom. 'Hey! Zack! Found it?'

The words zithered and skittered, like high-hysteresis globes: 'He -ey -ey! Zack -ack -ack!' 'Found it -oundit -oundit?'

'No -oh -oh!' Conrad yelled back, wishing the deadening floor would swallow the echoes, too. 'What chance do we stand -and -and?'

'If we don't find him,' Lawrence said through the echoes, 'we're all done for! Finished -inished -inished!'

Well, that was true enough. Distasteful though the concept must be to men of the stamp of Tony Lawrence and Zack Conrad, and repugnant though it might be for them to venture into this end of the city, they had to face those concepts and venture down here. If the crisis Sturm feared proved insoluble then they and their kind faced an extinction as definite as that of the dinosaur. Conrad, perhaps alone among his fellows, shrank from the prospect that others would write a notation on their story in the footnotes to history.

'No luck so far. . . .'

'Check over the far end. I've finished here.'

'Damn labels . . . Stupid workers. They'll never qualify for the whole sewn-up saga.'

Conrad fished a label around, wiped a thump across the dusty face. 'Nothing.' He squinted in the pearly washed-out light across at Lawrence. 'A sewn-up saga's a one-way trip.'

Lawrence ducked clumsily beneath a hammock sending it swaying. A woman's leg dangled down, scraping the floor irritatingly. 'So they say. But someone's supposed to have managed to return – why, beats me.'

'Stories,' said Conrad, flicking labels. 'I don't believe them. Nothing to come back to here. Any luck?'

'No.'

'He's not here then. Oh, damn and blast and saga the man! This is a foul dump, the dregs of the dregs. What by the light of LSD would he want coming here?'

11

'He goes everywhere – you know. Passim.'

The echoes made of 'Passim' a bee-buzzing swarm.

'Let's get out of here -ere -ere.'

Bludgeoning swaying hammocks out of their way the two men fought through to the exit. Golden sunlight slanted down into the ward, a golden miasma against lustreless pearl within, warm. Neither man noticed it.

Before moving into the sunshine Conrad stopped to scan the city end. He lifted the scanner – the model was old and trustworthy even if the gadget itself had only recently been manufactured and therefore must automatically be suspect – and panned it carefully across the scene.

He could detect no significant increase in any of the body-heat loci the scanner identified. Not that infra-red detection could any longer be trusted one hundred per cent, the concept had fruited and withered beyond its useful term; but now Conrad could not linger. Pressures dictated by personalities with whom he shared a permanent servitor relationship drove him on, so he said: 'A dozen people out there, Tony. No significant increase in body-heat. . . . '

'We'll have to take the chance. Make sure your badge shows nice and big.'

'Yes.'

Lawrence wore pale blue shirt and slacks; but his badge shone the same as Conrad's, over his left breast and large and unmistakable on his back. Their parents had naturally inducted them into their own Insurance Company and that was how they came to be friends.

Conrad didn't particularly like Lawrence. Not that he liked anybody, really, you just couldn't afford to, even your friends.

Lawrence smoothed a trusting hand over his Insurance badge on his chest. The complicated stitching and wired-in electronic circuits feeding from his heartbeat and respiration and brain, the gaudy symbols, the red cross, the swords, the tommyguns, the pious little symbols, too, all added up to security. Or, Conrad thought nastily, watching Lawrence fondling his badge, or as near as a man ever can get to security in these damned days.

'Come on, Tony. We'd better check the next dump. If he came down here he could have gone anywhere.'

'Yes.' Lawrence looked out over the deserted streets, the sun

12

glinting from windows and reflecting in bitter sword-strokes from shattered edges, the aridness of the scene. 'Yes. If he did . . . This frightens me, Zack.'

'It scares hell out of me, too, Tony. But you know what Sturm said.'

'Please.'

'All right. Come on then.'

They clattered over the concrete. They left the hospital behind them, skirting around the fallen west wing, the rubble looking like exhausted ruins of a forgotten time, crystallised in meaningless postures. They ran across a silent and motionless speedway, leaping the rusting junctions, feet hard and metaliic on the treads.

'There's a sign.' Conrad pointed.

Lawrence shaded his eyes against the sun. His blond hair and skin would mottle and blotch if he wasn't careful. His hand shook as he lifted it.

He was, Conrad saw with small humour, really frightened.

The sign purveyed its information with a dismal conformity to hundreds of others such signs in this end of the city. They approached warily, not used to the role Sturm had called on them to perform, uneasily aware that a sign might say what a hundred others said and still give a different meaning from what it said. Doing that little trick was a natural part of information dissemination. Trouble was – some people took a long time to realise and understand what was going on.

The sign said:

TRIPLINERS
NO WAITING—ONE HUNDRED COUCHES

'That is if he came in one of these tripjoints,' Lawrence said, worried, gnawing his lower lip. He couldn't handle his fear and Conrad, to his own disgust, felt a stab of pity for Lawrence. Hell! The guy was over twenty-one, wasn't he?

Just being out here, with the set-back buildings hemming him in from a distance and not crowding the pavements, set an itch in his brain, made him flinch back from any movement. The tall round-faced fronts of buildings seemed to grin down at him, nasty, knowing, crowding together but giving him ample elbow room, leaving him in an arena of pavement –

'Shall we go in?' Lawrence said.

13

Conrad's thoughts jangled – hell and all that – he'd been really going then! This place had got him going!

'Sure,' he said in a surly and none-too-steady voice.

He walked into the tripjoint through the sagging ever-open door sullenly. He knew Lawrence had seen him get going. He'd been taking a secret enjoyment from witnessing Lawrence's fear and then, like a striking snake, it had caught him up and stabbed him and the poison of fear had been working on him. He felt a fool. He didn't look at Lawrence. Hell – the guy would be laughing at him!

Zack Conrad, whose parents still talked to him, possessed a not unjustifiably exaggerated impression of his own worth. Even Sturm had bent a twinkling eye beneath a dominating eyebrow on him when this search through the city for Vincent had been suggested. So, as they walked with stiff precision into the tripjoint, Conrad felt the mental breeze of shamefacedness coursing through his mind. Lawrence could go and saga himself.

This place had been a theatre. Marble slabs snapped echoes back at them from shining walls. The paybooth repeated the information displayed on the outside sign. The steps beyond, their carpeting shredding and mouldering into purple efflorescence, led up into shadows.

'Come right through, sirs. No waiting! Luxurious couches – fumigated every hour on the hour! Step this way, sirs!' The old crone cackled at them like a schizophrenic maiden aunt, dribbling.

'We're not taking a trip . . . ' Lawrence began; but the hag, her anodised aluminium slacks tight around scrawny shanks and her glitter-look-see-bodice sagging over a shrunken chest, fastened one yellow-taloned hand on to his arm, staring up wild-eyed, her bleached hair tearing half-free from its beehive nesting of silver wires.

'Guaranteed the pure stuff, sonny! No artificials here, no pseudo's, no adulterants. . . . ' Her mechanical-gramophone voice scratched on along exhausted grooves. 'Just step right through, no waiting, pay as you go, no credits, only the best in the Cave of Aladdin's Perfumed Delights . . . No waiting . . . Come along, sonny. . . . '

Lawrence tried to free his arm. Her grip tightened.

Conrad, feeling nausea, said firmly: 'We must make an inspection.'

On the word the hag shrank. She flung Lawrence's arm from her, her face changing colour, thinning and tautening as of skin over a drumhead, her cracked lips quivering.

'Everything's of the best here,' she whined, defeated, her hands knuckling together loudly. 'We always see to the connections all right and proper.'

'I'm sure you do,' Conrad soothed her, and felt impatience with himself at the waste of time. 'It's not about that.'

Lawrence, rubbing his arm, his face pale, said: 'Why can't we just look in the auto places, Zack? I can't stand much more of this old woman.'

She repelled Conrad, too; but with his thoughts filled with images of Sturm, he could do nothing else but go on and obey his instructions. 'Come on, Tony,' he said roughly, pushing past and up the steps. The crone watched them go, her cracking knuckles like mourners' castanets behind them.

This was no do-it-yourself tripjoint like the abandoned hospital.

Here couches that on first inspection looked comfortable stood ranked in lines over the sloping floor where the rows of theatre tip-up seats had been ripped out. A vast bedraggled emerald green curtain hung down over the footlights, masking the stage. The air smelled close, with a hint of cloves. Only a few lights burned in ornate sconces around the walls.

Conrad and Lawrence began once more their hurried search. Here a face, wax and lax, twisted with inner tremors; there a face, taut and thought-garrotted, tense; on nearly all the couches faces partially reflecting the life of the drugged brains beyond looked like distorted reflections seen in a rippled pool. The faces' bodies sprawled on the couches, arms and legs in wide abandon, caught in the static pose of time-absorption, mindless.

'Hurry it up and let's get out of here,' said Lawrence.

Conrad, whose own tremors he felt sure must be sensed and cause Lawrence's contempt, nodded and went on searching. He fingered the plastic labels at the couch ends. Men and women who had raced into this place, into the Cave of Aladdin's Perfumed Delights, had spent no more time over jotting down their names than had those others in the hammocks of the Mary Roberts Ward. Finding the name Vincent was no more easy than recognising the wan, bearded, broad face of Vincent himself.

'Nothing here, Zack.' Lawrence had finished his side of the auditorium. Hurriedly, Conrad moved past the last few remaining couches, looking for a massy, spreading black beard, looking for the impatiently savaged word 'Vincent' on the plastic tags.

'Nothing,' he said when he stepped out into the aisle.

'Where the hell's the man got to!' exclaimed Lawrence with a peevishness that made Conrad want to laugh. The issues at stake made peevishness a childish pastime.

'Maybe someone else has found him, up at the other end of the city.' Conrad hoped this was true. 'Anyway,' he added in self-defence, 'he's more likely to have gone there. I can't imagine anyone coming down here.'

The look Lawrence bestowed on the Cave of Aladdin confirmed Conrad's own finicky judgment.

They walked back towards the exit where a sickly blue light glowed at half-power, passing the cables looping from each couch, climbing the slope with a little bent-over walk, anxious to reach the sunshine they hadn't noticed.

2

'Any hallucination is better than none!'

The words slipped towards him like a scimitar breaking brutally through the sky over his head and slicing the canvas of his world into shreds.

Across the still waters of the fjord the long half-submerged bulk of the island lay like an opaline smear. Its coral strand banding the water's edge bisected the humped shape of the island above and its reflection in the water below. Darkness shrouded the water, clouded the luminous path, deepened the pale green of the sky.

Stumbling against his own shadow away from that grinning mouth in the water, the island and its shadow, oyster-like mouth seeking to suck from his still-living body the life-juices of his ego, he bent and fled on – on. . . .

Colour burst on him. Dripping colour, fiery outlines, blazing palettes of light. The road turned scarlet, the trees orange and yellow and indigo. The lemon sky deepened into amethyst-flecked amber. Violet buildings wedged the horizon. A scattering of purple and crimson dots cascaded across his vision.

He reeled against the silence, pressing on.

Through the plastic soles of his shoes he could feel the pebbles, each pebble rounded and corrugated with its own surface roughness, the pimples and indentations on each corrugation piercing with separate and exquisite delicacy through his skin to impinge on the naked nerve endings of his feet. Touch scraped with the nutmeg-grater fineness of silk. He crooned silently to himself at the feather-strokes caressing his skin as the air rushed past, trailing scarlet and umber streaks.

The sky could no longer support itself under this outpouring of light and colour and silence. It collapsed inwards, rushing together, draining colour, leeching light, dragging down into darkness.

He cowered as the scimitar stroke slashed the sky.

He did not feel the prick of the needle; as always the first sensation was one of thirst, of a dryness that life could never slake.

'. . . better than none!' Griselda finished saying.

As usual the air of triumph about her had flushed her face and brightened her eyes. In her shapeless smock with the beer stains down the front she looked like an overgrown and semi-animated steel-engraving of a Tsarist peasant woman without any charm. Her cheeks shook as she spoke and speaking, laughed.

'Come along, Sheldon, do!'

He sat up creakingly, protesting witout heat. 'Plenty of time. There always is when you wake me.'

'There 's no call to be coarse, Sheldon.'

He wiped the backs of his hands over his eyes, looking about the hall. Of the seven beds only five including his own were occupied. Francis and Sammy lay on their backs, legs asprawl, mouths agape. Chloe and Doris lay on their sides, knees drawn up, bodies shapeless in vivid smocks like the one worn by Griselda. On the bed near the window overlooking the flats and the monorail where at this time of year the sun would strike in at half-past four. Deedee lay wantonly, her hair escaping from her hairnet and draping over the bedhead like a veil. Her smock had wrinkled and ruffled up past her knees and as Sheldon watched she turned lazily over, wriggling, so that the smock rose another six inches up her thighs.

Sheldon yawned again. He raised his fists and stretched. His face remained the blank sleep-immersed mask of the worker as Deedee turned voluptuously over, stretching like a kitten, and relaxed once more. He lowered his stiffly outstretched arms and thrust them, ramrod stiff, on to his knees, pushing hard. Then he yawned again and flexed his elbows and stood up.

He nearly fell and reaching back with a hand for support said: 'Whoops!'

'Come on, Sheldon!' Griselda pushed him aside with her

big soft body and flopped herself down on the warm bed. The crinkled sheets meant nothing to her as they had meant nothing to Sheldon. Deedee would see they were washed every now and then.

'I thought it was Sammy's turn?'

Griselda was reaching up to the shelf over the bed. She did not bother to turn her head as she said: 'Can't you think of a better one than that, Sheldon?'

'Well – he's always on a trip when I go and again when I wake up. So?'

'So!' She had found her own needle now. The westering sun gave it a little shine. She had no time to spare now for Sheldon or Sammy or any of them – no time for anything or anyone save the needle.

Sheldon raked around the floor for his slippers. This pad boasted linoleum on the floor and hook rugs scattered here and there. Sure, the wallpaper had long since stripped off; but the plaster still looked sound. At least, there were only two places it had fallen away from the laths. Sheldon, whose own bright red smock bore traces of beer and food, stumbled across to the window where the sink and tap showed stained brown and tarnished. He was still on that colour jag; his retinas echoed to the chromo-riotous trip.

He splashed water over his head and face and fingered his chin; his last depil should last for this shift and then, he promised himself, he'd fix another. He shook his head and admired the way water drops flew, motes of colour transparent in the sunshine one moment, solid and rounded tear-drops the next. He wiped himself here and there with a tissue and tossed it out the window.

Someone might collect it, sometime.

He felt that dryness and soreness in his throat and looked at the tap. That would run dry before he would be satisfied. He glanced across at the wooden cupboard on the wall beside Deedee's bed and decided he could hold out until he reached the canteen. His hunger appeared to him as fragmentary as the sunlight bouncing off the opposite wall where the clique hung their capes.

The badges shone coloured fire into the dingy room.

He noticed that Deedee had twisted around again. Her smock had burst a button at the neck and as he looked the

19

thread blew out like a gay streamer along her exhaled breath. She was wearing nothing underneath the smock. Deedee had asked to join their clique only recently – Sheldon was not sure just when or how long ago – and she was only about seventeen or eighteen with a trim white figure he had thought too slender for hard work.

He made a little tut-tutting sound with his tongue and moved over to Deedee's bed. Bending down, he pulled her smock over her knees and covered her breast. She stirred and her head lolled, her face with its indrawn look of sensuous pleasure, the closed eyelids tiny rounded mounds of flesh, the still-soft mouth with two ivory teeth-tips showing pressing into the rose-red lips, seemed to stare up blindly; hungrily at him.

He knelt down and found the button, carefully placed it on Deedee's shelf next to her needle.

Then, putting on his cape, he went out of the door and down the dark echoing stairs with their harsh concrete treads, to the street and work.

Below him the watchfires of the unappeasable dead glowed each like a devil's eye through the vorticing blackness.

His feet gripped with futile prehensile bluntness at the single bare plank. The wind whose teeth flayed with a cellular deconstruction of tissue blistered and blustered at his whipped body.

He knew that in less than a second he must fall.

Unless he could shift reality, refocus the plane of the hallucination, in some desperate way not at all clear to him remould the experience through which he was being unwillingly dragged, he would fall to his death.

Many a man under the prick of the revivifying needle had remained cold and lifeless. The thought nerved him, sent the blood in thick gushes from his heart, firmed down his trembling lips.

Abruptly, too fast for him to see without retentive vision, streamers and blobs, amoebas, cillas, molluscs of fire and light and colour poured past in a convulsive wave of transmuting forms, a skipping succession of half-realised shapes and forms, foaming.

He shrank back and his right foot slipped on the plank.

His fingers dragged like amputated stumps at the door at his back, locked and bolted, unopenable. He decided, rationally, calmly, that he had no wish any further to call himself Wendell. He would be – ah, yes! – he would be Higham.

He still wore cheap pyjamas. He was still wet through. But he no longer stood on a single plank above an unguessable gulf where the balefires of a poisoned host waited throatily.

Higham stood on the lush and luxurious pile of a carpet that could have softened the tread of a Marie Antoinette. Elegant Louis Sixteenth furniture stood about the vast chamber beneath crystal chandeliers. Their soft waxen light lit up brilliantly the painted ceilings, carved and gilded, delicately tinted, lavish and with a decadent softness of demi-Rococo. Pilasters of gilt and ivory separated vast paintings of mythological scenes – Diana and her maiden huntress, Pygmalion and Galatea, the Toilet of Venus – in which the rosy flesh of the women glowed down in lush abandon.

Higham stood dripping on the carpet, his head tilted back, his mouth half open, his massive beard bristlingly cocked, admiring.

'François Boucher, those are,' said a voice close to his elbow. 'Pretty-pretty stuff – but fun.'

Higham looked down, prepared for anything.

He saw a short roly-poly little man with a yellow face that smiled much too easily, pince-nez and dabby little grey wings of hair rising on either side of an emerald green skull cap. He appeared to be dressed – Higham could not be completely sure – in half-armour and silken breeches and hose, with socks in the toes of which large holes revealed plump toes and shiningly manicured toenails.

'You can't take it all seriously,' he rambled on, speaking in a melodious voice and walking – with a chiming clank of armour – across to a secretaire. 'But when you realise what it can do – you must take it seriously. Your whole livelihood depends on it. You do see, don't you?'

He turned suddenly to stare at Higham, tucking his head down and staring up so that his eyeballs rolled.

'Exactly,' said Higham firmly. 'There's rather a jumble of periods, though.'

'Naturally. We have to cater for all tastes. Take this sec-retaire, now. Beautiful piece. A Martin Carlin, Louis Six-

teenth. Look at the panels, Sèvres porcelain. Incredible –
useless – but lovely.'

'Everyone to his own taste,' said Higham, looking about for
a chair he would not desecrate by sitting in. 'I prefer gunmetal
and sliding drawers and filing cabinets. But then, I have large
quantities of papers to which to refer.'

'That must be an inconvenience for you.'

He had to remember he was Higham now. Wendell was
gone. He tried to bring back to memory why he had decided to
adopt a different name at that point. The pressure of the
moment – the fires, the height of his coming fall, the darkness
and terror – all had pressured him into taking the only step
that could save him. There had been no flicker of ingrown
emerald and amber and ochre squares, no typical transition
phase. One heartbeat he had been *there* – the next – *here*.

He sat down in a walnut construct that, cunningly, proved
most comfortable. The comforting warmth of the room was
drying him out; but still his pyjamas dripped water. He did
not feel cold.

'I am happy to welcome you here.' The small yellow face
smiled knowingly. 'My name is Comfort. Perhaps I could get
you some refreshment? Some tea or coffee? Or – ?'

'Yes, please,' said Higham, accepting it. 'Something a little
stronger.' He lifted a thick wet fold of the pyjamas wadded
from their thin tissue. 'And perhaps you'd be good enough to
lend me some clothes.'

'Of course,' said Comfort, nodding. 'My pleasure.'

Higham did not see Comfort ring but the next second a girl
glided in carrying a tray with whisky and glasses. She was
followed by another girl carrying a white nylon shirt and dark
grey trousers, underwear and carpet slippers. Both girls wore
bikinis and flowing transparent veils; both were redheads;
both were extremely well-developed.

Higham looked with relish.

Comfort clapped his hands.

The two girls undressed him, towelled him, dressed him. It
all took about two minutes flat.

'Sit there and relax and drink your whisky,' Comfort said
with a benign smile, clapping his hands and despatching the
two redheads. As they went the second one looked back over

her shoulder and winked at Higham. He lifted his glass to her.

'What time is this?' said Higham, at ease with his whisky in the chair. He knew his hallucinations better than most people – after all he created the things – but he had been badly shaken by finding himself in pyjamas in a strange town in the night. He had no clear recollection of the events leading up to that hallucination. He had, as he often did, gone downtown to sniff out what was happening and had tried, without a single qualm, Guztav Lawlor's Luxury Relax Palace. Then the pyjamas and the rain and the sleazy hotel and the stairs and the door and . . . Yes.

'Time?' said Comfort, climbing via a beaded footstool into a chair opposite Higham's.

'Yes, you know. Year, century, date.'

'I don't believe you'd understand.'

Higham had started on what he usually said. 'Oh, I was just interested to know what the date was – ' Then he paused. 'What did you say?'

'I don't believe you'd understand.'

'Surely you mean: "I don't believe I understand?" don't you?'

'No.'

'Oh.'

Comfort had been provided with a cut-glass decanter which contained a ruby red liquid. This he poured slowly and with relish into a squat cut-glass tumbler, the edges of the glass catching reflections of light and ruby colour to make a maze of crimson. Comfort lifted the tumbler with sincere appreciation. 'You see,' he said over the rim to Higham. 'We're outside time here. Well, we'd have to be, wouldn't we?'

Whether to agree or argue had always presented an interesting dilemma to Higham; but he said simply: 'Oh, I suppose so, if you say so, Comfort. But I like to anchor myself in the space-time continuum, you know.'

'I do know, Bung.' And Comfort drank to him.

In politeness Higham had to answer with a lift of the glass before Comfort drank.

'So this place has no existence outside my own imagination, then?'

'I wouldn't say that. A trifle – drastic, wouldn't you say?'

'Solipsism with megalomaniac trimmings?'

'You could do worse, of course.' Comfort rolled the large squat glass between his child-like hands. 'Your own world is in one hell of a mess right now.'

'Do you think I don't know that? I'm not altogether happy about Sturm. He is trying to act out his part as autocrat. And the drugs lately haven't been giving prognosticated results. But we soldier on.'

'Soldier. Yes. You've finished with wars, haven't you, in your real world?'

'Of course. The Age of Material Plenty could not tolerate warfare. The archaism insulted a scientific and humanistic intelligence.'

'But not an ambitious one.'

'I don't believe Sturm has a single such notion in his head.'

'I believe you. So will thousands of others. But, perhaps, millions won't.'

'Rubbish!'

Comfort laughed with malicious gentleness and tossed off the rest of the drink. He stood up with pygmy energy.

'Come along, then. Let me show you your room.'

'You expect me to stay?'

'Where else would you go? As long as you are Higham, that is.'

'I see.'

The large double-panelled folding doors drew back as they approached across the ocean of carpet. Comfort hopped along with the agility of a cricket. His armour, whose reflections mirrored the splendours of ceiling and walls in contorted ripples of colour drowned in steel, clanked pleasingly. His socks offended Higham; but he felt he could not comment on his host's personal appearance. There were bounds beyond which a gentleman, however drug-sodden he might be, would not step.

Drug-sodden.

Well, so was everyone else and seeing nothing unusual in it. The Age of Material Plenty had brought more than material comfort; it had brought problems only dimly sensed in the affluent, happy, couldn't-care-less civilisations of the twentieth century. If those selfish people living then had looked more closely at the people of India and Africa and China, and more closely at bonanzas of natural gas estimated to last fifty years, instead of ignoring the one and thinking the other would last for ever, much of the world into which he had been born would have been more pleasing to a man with a conscience.

'Let 'em stew!' he said with a savageness that brought the words into audibility on his lips.

Comfort stopped at once, half-turned, his peculiar wide clownish face upturned. 'Yes?'

'Nothing. Just thinking that we'd be happier now if those idiots hadn't used up natural resources so fast, if they'd looked to the salvation of their own souls more than the lining of their pockets.'

Comfort's level gaze mocked him. 'I had no idea you were a Moral Aid firebrand!'

'I'm not!' Higham felt disgusted with his own point of view, however much he could see its apparent strength. 'I've heard what they say and I've seen their shows. But I don't know. Maybe those old folk weren't all as bad as that. I mean – they did invent the processes that still feed and clothe us, didn't they?'

'You ask yourself the question, Higham. I am merely a clown called Comfort.' And his smile did not vary a muscle-tremor as he led on down the carpeted corridor.

The world was the world. Higham had been born into it, more by luck than judgement, had studied and had mastered his craft. He accepted what he saw about him as what he saw about him, which made his hallucinations that much easier to enjoy. Like now. Comfort threw open a door into a bedroom, a wide tall room with narrow windows and much gilding and decoration and painted pictures that, if not obscene, were near enough erotically stimulating to cause him pleasure without the taint of childish muck-raking corruption that made of obscenity a ludicrous farce.

'Your room, Higham. Daphnis or Chloe will be here as soon as you ring.'

'Which one was – ?'

'Daphnis. Her wink, I am told, is a marvel of perfection.'

'She will suit perfectly.'

Hesitating, Comfort turned back. 'If you wonder why she bears the name of an unhappy shepherd son of Hermes in-stead of the chaste daughter of the river Peneius, your answer must lie in the escape of the one from Apollo when he tried –

well, what you no doubt intend shortly to perform yourself.'

Vague memories of childhood rushed back on Higham.

'Hermes,' he said, rolling the names around his tongue. 'Daphne. Yes, I remember – '

'She will not disappear and fob you off with a laurel, she knows her art very thoroughly indeed.'

'I, at least, can be sure of that, since this is my hallucination.' Despite himself, Higham could not keep the pompousness out his voice.

Comfort chuckled, an elfish gurgle of good-humour, and took himself off.

Higham strolled into the room, pressed the bed's mattress and assured himself the springiness was all that could be desired. He felt in remarkably fine spirits. This was more like normalcy. Old Guztav Lawlor, despite his situation in the sleazy downtown area, could be relied on. Higham, whistling an indifferent little tuneless snatch, started to take off his shirt.

A noise reached him from the door and he turned around, smiling.

Her midnight-blue gown a flame of electric brilliance in the Rococo bedroom, the leopard woman with wasp-like eyes glided towards him. She no longer carried her four-foot long tail in her gloved and jewelled hands; the tail rippled behind her and, even as Higham stared, appalled, it straightened. Her scarlet nails glistened. Her angel's face smiled with syrupy sweetness. She moved towards him, pressing him back on the bed with very deliberate intent.

3

The late summer sunshine laid butter-thick slabs of yellow across the concrete road. Even the rusted treads of the speedway glowed with an orange lustre. No trees grew in this downtown area where the building rounded their fronts on to the pavements, each a massive block crowding its neighbour and leaving open and vasty spaces between speedway and sidewalk, pavement and opposite building.

Zack Conrad checked his scanner for increased body heat anywhere out there across the inhospitable expanse.

Lawrence, at his side, cocked an eye.

'No significant increase again, Tony. Maybe it will be all right again.'

'If it isn't our badges – '

'Our badges!' Conrad wanted to feel the same aura of protection from his badge as very obviously and hungrily Lawrence took from his. The badges were the same, identical in makeup, each one keyed to the life-rhythms of its owner and ready to trigger abnormalities back to Insurance Towers. The differences lay in colour and design as from Company to Company, and, as a necessary corollary, a difference in the Insurance Company to which the information of death or injury would be sent.

As they said when they induced you: 'It's nice and reassuring to know that if you are killed you will be avenged!'

Conrad put the scanner away, touched his badge lightly, and stepped out away from the Cave of Aladdin's Perfumed Delights.

'Where now, then?' demanded Lawrence petulantly.

Conrad regarded him with half an eye, his most important

task now was to insure their safe arrival at their next investigation point, and Lawrence's pusillanimity while amusing him also angered him. He forgot his own crisis of nerve of a moment ago.

'Look for a sign,' he said curtly. No nudism could be possible between this man and himself, he reflected, and took a sardonic satisfaction from the thought. At least, he corrected himself as he walked quickly over the motionless treads of the speedway, no other newdism between their psyches than one of hostility and contempt.

The receding profiles of the buildings, whose outlines massily converged in a distancing blueness, formed avenues of sky framed by palisades of concrete, steel and glass. Very little movement could be seen. Many of the towers had fallen and spilled their masonry across the pavements like discarded alphabet blocks. The absence of greenery, the void left by the complete exclusion of natural growing plants and flowers, created, in Conrad, an ache for something he could not recognise. He was, he could never really comprehend, a full human being manqué.

The two men stepped quickly over the speedway and across the central lane. All to the side of the theatre lay in jumbled ruins. They must skirt back past the hospital with its ravaged west wing, and go on from there. In the luminous amber sunshine and the grape-purple shadows their figures threw back a harsh clash of colour, jagged and sharp, flamboyant.

They walked warily and Lawrence kept his right hand permanently on the butt of his gun. Conrad kept looking ahead, trying to orient himself with the map Sturm's hypnocartographer had imprinted on his brain. Beyond the next intersection the flying apparently unsupported archways of the abandoned monorail sprang leopard-like across their field of view. A scrap of blue sky showed beneath, making of the flyover a stained white architrave.

As they walked on half a dozen men and women walked slowly from a block of apartments on their right, began to cross the road, their feet loud on the treads of the speedway.

Lawrence jerked his gun out. He almost dropped it. He fiddled with it in sweaty palms. He swallowed twice, convulsively, and his knees bent.

'Put the gun away, Friend,' advised Conrad. 'They are

28

workers and you don't have to ask which way they are going.'

Lawrence contrived to put the gun in its holster on the third attempt. He licked his lips. 'Going – going to work. Sure. Well, they need a swift kick to help them on their way.'

Conrad agreed.

Alertly, walking like stalking cats, and yet pretending to be unaware of the workers, Conrad and Lawrence moved along the pavement. The sun's disc hung now halfway down the sky and shadows stretched stout and purple, surrounded by too much diffused brightness to appear a true black. The air smelt fresh, raw, nerve-wracking to nostrils tended by air-conditioning.

The dozen or so workers passed beneath the base of an intact building – a surburban factory unit by its functional design. Down at this end of town other buildings had been left over even from the times before the new era of Material Prosperity. These endo-skeletal buildings appeared hard and cold, crowding, cumbersome, antediluvian, compared with the exo-skeletal homes and apartments of the Upper end of town. No lightness and grace appeared there to Conrad's eyes, only heaviness and ugliness.

That heaviness served merely to emphasise the ghastly openness of downtown for Conrad.

Expecting to see the workers reappear, Conrad felt that little jolt of dis-orientation when they failed to walk out of the shadow into the probing sunshine. He shaded his eyes. Then, swiftly, he snatched out the scanner and held it up.

'Get down, Tony!' he shouted in panicky reaction.

Lawrence threw himself to the ground, and then rolled over until he could hide himself behind a concrete outcropping of the speedway. Conrad joined him. Damned meter shows increased body heat right up into the hundreds!'

'Can you see anything?' demanded Lawrence. He did not offer to look over the concrete slab himself.

'Give it a moment.' Conrad's hands were still shaking.

'I'm not cut out for this kind of thing.'

'It's happening all the time out here, so they say.'

Somebody ran fleetly from the shadows of the factory building, sliding through the falling wedge of sunlight between walls like a goldfish, flicked into darkness again.

Conrad licked his lips.

'I don't know what's going on,' he said snappishly. 'But the infra-reds showed increased body-temperatures out there and that means trouble.' He hunkered down beside Lawrence. 'We ought to stay here for a bit, Friend.'

'I'm not arguing, Friend.'

Not for the first time Conrad thought how lucky Lawrence was to be a member of his own Insurance Company, overlooking the obvious truism that had he not been Conrad would not have had the same opportunity to come to detest him. You were saddled with your Friends by the Company. To injure a Friend was to injure yourself: protection operated within the framework of social security as well as without.

He checked his hypnotically implanted map again. If they could skirt back around the toppled west wing of the hospital they could cross into a parallel avenue and make their way south again. Once past this locus of trouble facing them they could swing back once more into this avenue and continue their search. Whoever Sturm had sent to search the parallel avenue – Pearl Avenue, it was – wouldn't object to them trespassing momentarily.

Lawrence fell in with the scheme at once. They began to crawl back trying to keep the concrete outcropping between them and the shadows buttressing the factory building. Conrad scraped his knees and swore. Neither of them was very adept at this sort of undignified contortion.

After a few yards they could stand up in a crouched over position and so run into the rubble-strewn alleyway beside the hospital. No bullets cracked after them.

'Local fight,' panted Lawrence, hurdling fallen masonry.

'Louse-ridden workers aping their betters,' Conrad said, ashamedly conscious of the itch that had fretted away at his spine, too, during that dash for cover.

Of the two reasons for that that had popped into his mind only one fitted. He cursed Sturm sourly as he followed Lawrence up the alleyway.

Going like that, all fretful and impatient and ashamed of his cowardice, Conrad glanced down the slot of darkness at right angles to the alleyway, paralleling the avenue, to the oblong haze of afternoon sunshine at its end. He saw a sign there, etched in blue fire, discreet, held a little back from the line of the alleyway. The building could have been a church at one time or another; the fake-Gothic of cornice and pinnacle, buttress and battlement, soured a dark-grey note of bitterness into the rotting flamboyance of the surrounding architecture.

'There's a sign,' he said to Lawrence, halting and hesitating.

'I see it,' said Lawrence, going on strongly, not stopping.

'But we ought –'

Lawrence turned his head. His lips looked protruding purple ridges. His face sheened glassily, like the face of a pole-axed swimmer.

'You go down there if you like, Zack. Those worker goons went that way, you saw that.'

'I know . . . but –'

'Who's to know? Sturm won't even leave his room let alone come up here, and his spy eyes and bugs can't be operating in this alleyway – that's only common sense.'

'Well, yes, I suppose so.' Conrad had absolutely no desire at all in this world to walk down that slot of darkness to the blue etched sign at its end.

'We'll go through into Pearl Avenue and then cut back,' Lawrence said firmly.

Conrad followed. He could feel through the pores of his skin, so it seemed, the loathsome newdisms from the worker scum brawling down at the far end of that slot. No one of the upper end of town even knew now how many parlours and palaces and halls and relaxers there were proliferating around here in the lower end. Canned music and automated barkers had long since vanished from the narrow noisome slots of blatantly illuminated darkness. You went along to your favourite place and took a trip. Thinking like that made Conrad feel thirsty.

Not to go down towards that blue-fire sign crawling like Chinese firepaper seemed to Conrad the best of good sense. They had been assigned to investigate the Avenue of the Spheres. Resolutely, fixing his mind on the idea of reaching Pearl Avenue, of going along it for a block or so and then of cutting back into their own avenue, he crossed the mouth of the slot after Lawrence. Just before the crumbled wall of the building cut off the view he caught a last blue-glimmering glimpse of the sign.

The sign said:

GUZTAV LAWLOR
HIS LUXURY RELAX PALACE
CATERS ONLY FOR YOU

Sheldon wiped perfunctorily at his harsh red smock and, with fingers at least clean around their tips, jabbed his fingerprints on to the transparent plastic plate of the clocking-on machine.

Around him other workers – never fellow workers – stumped morosely past, faces scowling or frowning or drawn down in impatient thirst-lines. Their red smocks, no cleaner and no dirtier than Sheldon's, formed a corpuscle-tide pumping into the heart of the factory. For the factory drained, demanded, deadened. The factory took life. The factory kept men and women from their couches and from their dreams. The factory stole a part of their lives.

Sometimes Sheldon would talk to his nearest neighbour on the console; more often, like most of them, he preserved a prized anonymity. He had, he thought vaguely, only twice exchanged a newdism with a worker here, and both times had affected him unpleasantly. The first nudism had been with a young chit of a girl, the second newdism with a grey-haired man – he had recently arrived – and neither newdism had been complementarily sought; on both occasions Sheldon's thoughts had been digging deeper than he had realised.

The line moved on. Most often, like today, the workers clocked on with their prints to prove to Central Welfare they had arrived for work, maintaining throughout a sullen waiting silence. There was no need to talk in the factory. Automation handled the purely productive processes. Electronic circuitry handled the automation. The few human beings necessary initiated supply runs, made executive decisions, pressed a few buttons. The work, Central Welfare very often made a point of informing the workers, paralleled in effort and mental capacity that performed by the very highest echelons of business management and technology during the build-up phases to the era of Material Plenty. Sheldon, for example, he had been taught to think, held the same position and performed the same functions, as a President of an Incorporated Group of Companies controlling steeel, textiles and drugs of the late Twentieth Century. The capital letters spilled over in gobbets of light and fanfares of brass.

32

Big deal.

Sheldon wiped his nose on his fingers, wiped them down his red smock, and so settled himself into the plastic-leather chair at his Presidential desk.

Logan Transport over on the East Coast wanted more steel; they were having trouble shipping natural gas. Last time he had been on shift Sheldon had authorised a half-million ton swap with Scarfe Tubing, over-riding the instant protest of the automated quota system, cutting out the computerised calculations. Maybe some clever dick handling this set-up while Sheldon had been off shift had re-routed the steel, reallocated, cut the robot back into the deal. Cursing without feeling, a routine meaningless ritual mouthing, Sheldon checked.

He didn't care if Logan Transport never got their steel, never shipped any more natural gas for a lifetime. In a decaying economy who cared?

What Sheldon cared about, passionately cared about to the exclusion of everything else, was to get back to his couch and take a trip.

He hammered buttons, set up a re-run on the previous shift's operations, his mind perhaps a quarter occupied. Twining like autumn leaves of red and scarlet and amber, cascading down into his brain, the memories of his last trip rode always with him, both above and below the thresholds of this so-called reality about him. A vague feeling of unease troubled him as he recalled. Some tiny tickling feather of doubt perplexed him as he luxuriated back into that screaming world of colour.

Screaming. Yes. The colour impact had been nerve-eroding, paring his perceptions, the noise a multi-decibel yell of agony.

Not for the first time Sheldon, along with everyone else of his acquaintance, wished with dull resignation for personal control over the subjects, landscapes and impressions of a trip. He had once been on a trip where poetry had steamed at him from every orifice of giant shining brass machines, insane concentrics of wheel and spring revolving, and the poetry gushing forth like half stuff in a paper mill. Blinded by consonantal rhymes, deafened by assonances, his metre limp, he had staggered – during that trip – to fall with a soundless scream five hundred feet into the Erkansater end of a Fourdrinier and be washed and couched and calendered into a shining blankly receptive roll. He had enjoyed it all. Every second had been riotous fun. He had not, he felt sure, enjoyed the sight of that gargoyle mouth in the fjord, the coral road up which, against a vast and invisible wind, he had struggled bent over like a safety-pin. He just had not *enjoyed* his last trip.

This not only saddened him – the more he thought about it the more frightened he became.

The controls before him complained that he had routed a million novacamphor B eighty-one anti-cold pills to the tropics – and a demanding and acerbating red panel lit with the words: 'Request Immediate Return to Computer Control.'

'What the hell do I care for your stupid anti-cold pills!' he said aloud, shaken up and angry. 'Here!' He slapped the controls with vicious uncaring expertise. He just hadn't realised he'd hung on to manual when he'd finished that stupidity about the steel for Logan Transport.

Trivia of that nature were not part of a President's active concern; he would deal with matters after they had been settled by the computer, reading off the history on graphs.

If only work these days could demand more from a man!

Any half-educated idiot could decide on the basis of the information portrayed by the controls what were the best paths for industry and commerce over the whole shift period. Unit and digital decision-making machinery, operating on a yardstick of the shift as a six-hour standard, could handle most development. There had been rumours of problems too complicated for the digital systems to handle; Sheldon had never encountered any of those in his ten years in this factory.

He processed a flow of data and thereby handled merchandise that, valued in late twentieth-century terms would have totalled ninety millions of money, and with a yawn looked about for the pre-programmed coffee spot.

For some reason that escaped him he looked through the plate-glass separating his operating console from the next and saw a young girl slumped forward over her console, her soft dark hair disarranged over her cheek.

She did not move as he looked. Her head lay pressed hard and angularly against metal switches. Now he saw that her left arm hung down straight and limp from the shoulder.

The coffee spot had not arrived yet. Sheldon set the computer to decide its own fate for the next five minutes, stood up, and then, with a careful movement he again could not adequately explain, walked from his console cubicle into the next. The girl still had not moved.

This peculiar sort of experience had not occurred to him before and among the shifting and bellicose colours that flashed and sirened about in his skull he stood as though isolated from what was happening in his own mind. He swallowed and tried to think. The girl must have fallen and knocked herself out against the metal console. She wore one of the standard issue violet smocks, stained less than the average, and her arm hung down thin and white and frail.

He put a hand on her shoulder and pulled gently.

'Miss!' He spoke with a catch in his breath and had to swallow again before he could get the tone right. 'Miss! Are you all right?'

Although Sheldon only barely realised this, the question stood as a fine example of the usual inane remark. He shook her shoulder again and bent down to look into her face. Only then could he see the dark stain of blood seeping in a bloody trickle from her temple pressed against the dark metal. He put both hands on her shoulders, feeling the bones like twigs, and pulled her back into her chair. Her head lolled and he pushed in back to lie awkwardly – but without any skin-folding of neck – down on her left shoulder, the injured temple uppermost.

This occurrence assumed more and more importance the more Sheldon considered it.

He had positively to fight to hold on to the colours of his last trip. He looked at the girl and thought vaguely about staunching the dark flow of blood; it was only a scratch but the sight of the blood affected him acutely, as though it was a personal affront.

Somewhere around each console a first aid cabinet hung, of this he felt reasonably sure, although as a phenomenon of importance in his life it ranked along with the laundry. He looked about vaguely.

A man glanced over from the next console on the other side and then returned his face to his work, a face drawn and waxen with exhausted longing, the eyes like pits.

For Sheldon the sight of the worker made him conscious of his own hypnomanic action – but some consciously unfelt chord had touched a responsive chord in him, the birth of an unwanted newdism, half-aborted, half-viable – but there, distinct, formed, waiting – like everyone waited.

He lifted the girl's violet gown and dabbed clumsily at the gash in her temple. The blood felt thick and tacky. He let the stained hem of the garment fall, conscious that he might do more harm than good, trying to focus her face clearly through the languorous colours and sounds rioting in his head.

Her console illuminated that superior sneering red sign: 'Request Immediate Return to Computer Control.' Unlike his own reaction, she had given her console no go ahead switching, and so the robot had illuminated a further sign, an angry smoky-orange: 'Turn over to Computer NOW!' A bell began to ring in angry Pekinese barkings.

Because the noise and flashing lights distracted him unpleasantly, Sheldon switched the console over to the computer. The lights died sullenly and the bell gave a final admonitory ring.

'Get lost,' Sheldon said without really thinking about what he was saying. He looked again at the girl, feeling a puzzled sense of frustrated resentment.

Her face although lax and in repose wore a resigned expression conveyed more by the softly drooping set of her mouth, the unlined forehead, the absence of betraying wrinkles and skin blemishes. She seemed to be one of those young girls who are born to accept life. Her hair, very dark and long, lay in a bedraggled damp mass over her shoulder and its thick heavy richness showed clearly against the whiteness of her skin. The dark blood from her temple had oozed stickily across her cheek, giving a smoky gash of colour to her paleness, a brutal lash along innocence. On her soft lips a white froth had dried. As Sheldon watched she moved, her head rolled a little, her eyelids fluttered.

'Where – ?' she began and at once quieted.

She put a hand to her forehead and felt the tackiness of her temple. Her fingers were exceptionally long and slender, pale, the nails almonds of shining pink.

'You – ' began Sheldon.

She cut him off by saying quickly: 'It's all right. Don't be frightened. I am quite all right.'

She turned her head and tilted her chin and looked at him directly. He saw her face like an opening flower – he thought admiringly consciously of the image, so close to a recent trip experience – and he saw her eyes, violet, deep, enormous – and –

. . . They were thrust together, naked body against naked body, hip and thigh and breast conjoining in a netsuke of white abandoned flesh, with all the jewels of Araby cascading down their backs, tinkling and chiming and raising wine-ripples below their dabbling feet. . . .

Both their minds recoiled from the newdism like tender flesh touching white-hot iron.

'I'm sorry – ' mumbled Sheldon, his emotions a mess.

'It's – ' she tried to say composedly. 'It's all right. Can you – ' She gestured helplessly.

He did not know what she wanted. He stood up and looked down on her in her plastic-leather chair, sitting up shakily now, one hand smoothing down that heavy mass of hair.

'I think there is a medicine cabinet – somewhere – ' she said, her voice like a feather.

'Sure,' he said, jerkily. 'I don't know, though, where . . . '

The nudism – it had been that rather than newdism this time – had shaken him. When mind leaped the unguessable gulf between mind and – what? This was not telepathy, of that everyone was certain. It revealed deep processes going on automatically and frantically beneath the lowest depths of the subconscious mind, it pertained not to mind but to brain and body, the old, black, ancient drives that could never be revealed to the light of day. To understand a nudism would be to negate it.

He could still feel the sensation of her white body against his flesh, still the strands of empathy between them clung like thinning but stiffening cords of treacle, still the body reacted although the mind had long ago recognised that nothing physical had passed between them. Nothing physical, that is, that a mind would recognise. . . .

He shuddered as the last symptoms of the nudism sloughed from the unforgetting cells of his body, draining the remembrances from a mind above all that.

The girl stood up, grasped with one hand at her control desk, and her reciprocal shudder moved the violet smock into a brief turmoil. She, too, had received all the impact that Sheldon had. A nudism was a duality of experience by its very nature.

37

The drive to find the first aid chest had now become an obsessive demand to Sheldon. If he could find the medicine cabinet everything would be all right, like the girl had said.

With more effort than he had expended over anything he could remember in a very long time he searched around the console cubicle, looking without reason in any spot his eyes happened to light upon, a habit-formed man performing actions outside the scope of his training; but a man learning.

The novel thought occurred to him to say: 'I wonder why we weren't told where the cabinet is?' But he could not follow the train of thought through to a conclusion.

She had resumed her seat as though finding sustenance from a usual position in her world; but her eyes regarded him as he moved about, deep and dark and not too unkindly.

She had to lick her lips twice before she could say: 'Why did you – what made you – why'd you come in?'

He did not know the answer to that himself.

He pushed a filing cabinet away from the wall on rubber wheels, looking down and hoping to find the box behind the cabinet. 'I dunno,' he said, the words slipping uneasily from his mouth. He didn't look at the girl. 'I saw you – your head – the metal looked – it looked hard. . . . '

She touched her temple. 'It does hurt.'

Her words – supremely foolishly – spurred him to look more avidly. Curse the damn box! Then he stumbled over a white-painted cabinet with a red cross stencilled carelessly on it; the paint had run and dried in streaks. He kicked it aside, looking for the medicine cabinet. The white-painted door sprang open and a freezespray rolled out.

'There!' she said, leaning forward and pointing.

'I can see it!' he said with a return to a naturalness with her. 'You talk too much.'

'And you gawp too much,' she replied at once, bristling, like a cat.

He walked across to her and handed the freezespray over. Her fingers touched his on the can . . .

. . . Steaming jungle, lianas, trailing fronds, gorgeous pallid flowers, the scent of rottenness in their nostrils – the crotch of the tree, bark rough beneath them, frangipani in her hair, black and lustrous and wound around her waist – her mouth red and juicy coming closer. . . .

He stumbled back, flinging one hand up before his face. She slid from the chair, dropping the freezespray with a clang to the floor. Both their faces scoured of feeling like skulls.

'You horrible little worm!' she burst out, shaking and sobbing.

'You miserable pot!' he shouted back, livid and frightened. 'Why don't you saga yourself!'

Then – then even as he looked at her . . .

. . . Softness caressed him, soft hands, soft hair, soft breast, soft lips – her face gigantic before him, crooning, welcoming, the eyes violet flowers of enjoyment, her whole being a single joyous yielding delight. . . .

The jolt resembled the jolt you got from an exposed cable end when electric current surged from it. . . . It was like taking a trip to end all trips. . . . It was like . . . Sheldon – single-name Sheldon – had no words to describe what he felt as the nudism clamoured to open his mind to what the secret cells of his body already knew and sang. . . .

'Is it a sewn-up saga?' the girl breathed, her face now flushed with blood beneath the skin, alive and vibrant and contrasting oddly with the drying darkening blood on her face.

Sheldon picked up the freezespray can. He held it out again. 'I don't know,' he said. 'Here.'

Normally, he would have added: 'Your face looks a bloody mess.' But now for some reason – after the nudism – he did not say the natural thing, did not make the obvious remark.

She took the can and their fingers did not touch. She sprayed the freezer over her temple, killing the pain, sterilising the wound, preparing the cells to grow fresh skin quickly. He stood back, looking at her.

She walked in a peculiar way, he noticed, as she returned the can to the white-painted cabinet. Her left knee tended to tuck itself in and behind her right knee, the leg bent and trailing a little, so that she walked with a scuffling swing, her hips going up and down in an oddly rhythmical way that appeared ungainly and laborious. Sheldon had never seen anyone walk like that before and the sight excited him.

The ever-present memories of his last trip that stayed circling and zooming in his mind dimmed and faded perceptibly. He looked at the girl more clearly than at any time before. He saw the pure oval of her face, the deep violet eyes, the redness of

39

her small pouting mouth, the roundness of her legs, their sheen and smoothness as she walked laboriously back to her chair. He saw the dark mass of her hair, heavy and long and dense, thrown back languidly as she moved her head to return his stare.

'What – ' he said, amazed at his own thoughts. 'What's your name?'

Her shock showed. She blinked. Her face lost much of that high colour, that betrayed unnatural high colour.

She hung her head so that her hair fell forward like a midnight waterfall, hiding her face. He caught her words, soft and scarcely uttered. 'I'm Minch.'

4

Higham's previous dealings with cat-women had been brief and to the point.

He had shot them.

Just why they should form a motif in his private hallucinations he had never felt sufficient interest to explore; but, he promised himself with some acerbity, if they persisted like this he would damn well take steps – long steps and ones calculated to do a most serious injury to the cat-women-forming chemical in his brain.

Just because she mewed softly and showed her claws in an hallucination meant that she must be taken just as seriously – more so – than if the man calling himself Higham-for-now had met her in what the world termed reality.

Hallucinations could kill even more surely than a bullet.

The midnight-blue gown spangled with sequins as she moved voluptuously towards him, bending over him, bearing down on him. Each scarlet nail caught a gleam of light and glistened as though already stained with a drop of his life blood. His throat felt cold and naked.

With slow mesmeric force she pressed him back on the bed.

The man who had called himself Wendell, then Higham, felt once more that pulsing need for change. The time drained away.

'I'm so grateful,' she purred at him. The half-mask she wore over her face concealing her forehead and nose and revealing the brilliance of her lips glinting in mock sympathy. 'I thought you would lo-ove room twelve A. So cosy. So warm.' She purred with a harsh delicate clicking.

Higham blanked her off with a feeling he tried not to recognise as desperation. He felt like an underwater swimmer caught in weeds. He would be – he would be – ah, yes – Dobel.

Slashing scarlet claws lacerated empty air – he saw the pestiferous things in the same instant they vanished.

The man who was called Dobel – clad in grey slacks, slippers, a white nylon shirt he was in the act of taking off – stood in the foyer of an exclusive restaurant filled with the murmur of polite conversation, the odour of fine foods, the scent of costly cigars, and through the sloping windows he could see the roofs of skyscrapers and the smoke and sun-glitter of a great city.

He thought he must be in the Skylite Room of the Satellite Tower.

Above his head metallic sculptures contorted against the sky, entwining space, defining the limits of life, black and silver and angular. The engineers called them aerials; but men of sensibility recognised in them different truths.

These geometrical shapes in metal, curvilinear, domed, rectangular, reticulated, moved slowly like gravity-defying mobiles, their constructivist forms following a perpendicular axis, their anti-doctrinaire motifs expressing clearly their role in the metropolitan society.

The engineers – poor souls – used them to channel signals to and from the earth satellites sweeping around the world.

Below Dobel's feet intricate electronic machinery worked mechanically and blindly away handling communications from half a world, flinging them up to the twenty-four hour orbit satellites, receiving back the answers in time.

All this gobbling of signals and inputs and feedback and gain and modulation told Dobel that this hallucination had roots in reality, the frenetic decaying reality of the latter end of the twentieth century. The Skylite Room, the restaurant perched atop the Satellite Tower, eternally revolving, giving grandiose views of skyscrapers below, could have been a conception only of brains obsessed with the coming importance of material prosperity.

Anywhere in the city where a view was not masked by a glass and plastic cliff you could see the Satellite Tower. Wherever you were it seemed to lean over towards you. The top bulged with the revolving restaurant and on a fine day the windows kindled with spraying fire, rotating a flashing sign proclaiming the gospel of prosperity.

Below in the narrow alleys with their neon signs and their come-on photos the sleazy Strip Acre pandered to sick minds. In broad daylight greasy-faced men stood in doorways, at their sides window displays of the dubious wares within, calling to passers-by with their offer of a drink and a strip, all very cheap – cheap and quick.

And the Tower soared above it all and stood as the symbol.

In the time in which Dobel really belonged, where he lay in Guztav Lawlor's Luxury Relax Palace, the Satellite Tower had long since fallen. Most of it had been cleared up.

But the taint of the gospel of Material Plenty still lay a heavy and souring breath to sear his world.

He shrugged his shirt back on. His face with its arrogant square of black beard tilted up. He felt tense. In any normal hallucination he would have simply walked into the restaurant knowing that although his dress should have barred him, in his own hallucination he could do as he pleased. But now he hesitated. He knew well enough the social pitfalls laid for the unwary feet by the cruel and frightened classes of the past. And he now knew with pitiless clarity that this was no normal hallucination.

Perhaps an adulterant had slipped into Guztav Lawlor's equipment – the drugs themselves were thoroughly tested out before ever leaving the government warehouses. He wanted very much to find out what might happen. If this hallucination could project incidents of a nature over which he – he! – had no direct control, then it was his duty to discover the causes. Anyone, even the most unskilful, could dream up something nice when they went on a trip. But if a new and ugly element had been added the whole social structure of his own time would be shattered, and some silly little microbe Guztav Lawlor had failed to disinfect from a needle might be the cause. . . . His mind, he realised with an amused shock, was rambling. Ahead lay a new adventure.

The steam-bath atmosphere of the place with its warm pink welcome might in other circumstances have revolted him. Decadence had always smelled of rottenness to him; although he knew that decadence to others meant release and excitement and a reason for living. In the pursuit of one's duty, though, Dobel told himself sternly – giggling behind the mind that framed the thought – one must pursue paths perilous and unpleasant.

He went in.

A soft-faced blonde in a scarlet sequined sheath dress walked in an ankle-wobbling sway over to him and lifted a glass soda-water siphon. She squirted him all over his chest and beard and face. Giggling, she swivelled away.

He wiped a finger down his eyebrows and nose and wrung out his beard.

A major-domo wearing a classically cut frock coat, top hat and aertex pants, a dignified chili-bom-bom, motioned Dobel to a seat. He sat where indicated. On the white linen napery a vast bowl of pink roses, their petals falling softly, one by one, concealed the view beyond. He knew anything could exist beyond the roses. People cried for the last rose of summer; but millions of roses lay ready to bud in the future.

A waiter – conventionally dressed – offered Dobel the menu.

He took it, and sighed, and thought of Daphnis, now one with the sands of unreal time.

He ordered crab done in the restaurant's own peculiar and special way, and a wine he felt inappropriate as a gesture of defiance at the culinary kings gourmandising their creative talents in the kitchens. 'Marsala?' said the wine waiter, snapping a clothes-peg over his wine-list. 'Certainly not.'

Fury shook Dobel.

'Why not, confound you?'

The wine waiter looked to be a shrivelled, bent-over, humourless little man with a tic in his left eye and a wart under his chin, just above his butterfly collar.

'Because you can't have Marsala with just any old dish.'

'I want it and I'm going to have it – and you call me "sir" confound your squinty-eyed incompetence.'

'I shall call the head waiter.'

The wine waiter gestured like a bird seeking a fresh crumb. The head waiter – like a penguin who knew the alphabet backwards – hopped up, his smile a dark insult.

'And what is the trouble, Alphonse?'

The wine waiter snapped his clothes-peg offensively.

'This – man – insists on Marsala with his bread and cheese. Anyone of any breeding knows you may drink only beer with bread and cheese. Draught beer.'

44

'Certainly, Alphonse, you know the obligations of gastronomy, none better.' The head waiter bent a condescending, a pitying, eye on Dobel.

'Now then, sir. What is your version of the story?'

That 'sir' did it.

Dobel stood up.

'This,' he said with level heat, 'is my hallucination. I run things here.' He picked up the bowl of blown roses and threw it at the two waiters. They both bent lightly at the knees, caught the bowl, and looked up as though awaiting applause. ' 'Owzzatt!' They both shrieked together.

Dobel flung away from the table, feeling his hunger lifting like a cobra-head, sniffing emptiness.

A red-headed girl wearing a green scintillating sheath dress swayed towards him. She lifted a soda-water siphon.

Before she could depress the lever and drench him, Dobel seized the siphon and turned it on her. She stood under the spray, twirling about, lifting her arms up, her body tight and taut. As the soda-water hit that magnificent green dress it shredded and crumbled away and ran like porridge to the floor.

Dobel hurled the siphon from him. He couldn't win. He knew that. Logic here twisted itself around so that everything he did ricocheted off at an angle, twisting his logic around a tesseract of unreason.

'You are leaving?' enquired the major-domo, with solicitous charm. He stood by the door, holding it open for Dobel with his left hand. His right hand held a plaster model of a man's hand, cupped, extended, the palm two-feet across, the fingers all of three feet long, nine inches thick.

Dobel looked down. 'I'm afraid I can't read your palm today, my good man,' he said with cold politeness. 'Go soak your head and come back same time tomorrow.'

The major-domo dropped the plaster hand. Its outstretched middle finger struck Dobel's toe through the slipper. He jumped as the pain lanced.

He couldn't win.

This hallucination might have been enjoyable in the sheer illogicality of its antics; but the undertones worried him. Clearly, here, a pattern was forming, a pattern of obstruction and insolence and of dog-in-the-manger denial of pleasure.

Everything he did not only twisted itself about logically; but logic itself had been brought in to deny him the allowable fruits of his dreams.

The sensation was that of feeling a misty cloud almost unseen cutting off the rays of the sun. . . .

He was being made to feel small.

Shiny emerald and dull ochre and glistening brown squares, interpenetrating, dancing, moving like castanets about and around within their frame descended before him. Oscillating rapidly the curtain whisked aside. Dobel hesitated, unwilling to take a step forward until the transition had finished; these phases could be difficult and could precipitate him bodily from the Satellite Tower – if he was still there.

This transition, unlike the previous interplay of shimmering squares, had fruited. He had time-shifted and space-shifted. He stood, still wearing his grey slacks and white nylon shirt and carpet slippers, in a crowded street. People and vehicles rushed past him. Carbon monoxide stank in the heavy air. The evening light cast a ruddy, swimming colour over the busy scene; the square-outlined cars with ridiculous pseudo-space ship fins and vulgar stretches of chromium-plating, the hurrying forward-thrusting people with sooty clothing, all seemed as though lightly brushed over with salmon-pink paste.

Nearer mid-twentieth century now, Dobel thought, a feeling of distaste souring the expectation.

He glanced up in case the Satellite Tower might still be there but saw only the hazy outlines of buildings dark against a dark sky; windows in mindlessly severe rows lit with the last of the artificial daylight within, before six o'clock brought universal extinction. The thick air tasted furry. Noise of engines and horns and bells insulted the ear with trivia.

The frost in the air annoyed him as well; one detail he always insisted on was warmth and comfort within his own hallucination. But – was this his own hypnotic world any longer? People pushed past; boys and girls young and arrogant let out from offices, older men and women saddened by the sameness of days, buying their evening paper, racing for the subway, lining for buses. He stood alone, unwanted among the crowd.

Along the edge of the pavement towards him shuffled an old, decrepit and hairy man, his hair like a lion's mane outstretched and angry. He wore clumsy boots tied with string, baggy and shiny trousers of a colour dyed by the years, a rusty coat buttoned tightly. He carried strapped over his shoulders and hanging down front and back a sandwich board, and the billboard extended above his head on pseudo-classical columns. The boards waggled and swayed as he shuffled along, making the thick and demanding print difficult to read.

Sunken in hair, the man's face consisted of a round fleshy knob for a nose, high-ridged and ruddily-shining cheekbones, a sunken gulf for a mouth and eyes peering from overhanging eyebrows.

Dobel automatically moved aside to let the sandwich man pass.

REPENT YE!
GOD'S DAY OF JUDGEMENT
IS AT HAND!

Dobel had to skip back a pace to allow the boards to swing past.

REPENT YE
WHILE THERE IS YET TIME
FOR THE THINGS OF THE FLESH
SHALL UNDO YE AND THE THINGS
OF THE SPIRIT SHALL SAVE YE.

Dobel nodded. Succinct, unsubtle and straight to the point. The message reminded him of the Moral Aid cranks of his own reality.

As the man passed he swivelled an eye at Dobel and the stitched mouth opened vacantly.

'Repent ye!' said the man in a tubercular voice. 'Give up your fornication and your gluttony, give over your whoring after the material things of life! For I say unto you – '

The message was never delivered, at least to Dobel and at that time, for a spasm of coughing took the hairy sandwich man and he bent so that the upper board swayed like the collapsing sail of a frigate shot away in an engagement. He coughed and spat scarlet.

'Get away you filthy beast!' a young girl's voice said.

She drew her skirt away around her cheap nylons, her card-

47

board shoes cracked across the insteps. Her escort, a young man with a cigarette hanging from his lips – a sure sign, Dobel knew, of a retarded mentality – pushed her aside. His face showed a flicker of animation.

'Watch it, mac!' he said with cinematic expertise.

The old man coughed his life blood out on to the hard concrete.

Dobel had no time for anyone here. In their own ways each was insane, each an imperfect part of a whole that offended him. The youth took out a handkerchief and blew his nose meaningfully at the old man, then stuffed the handkerchief back into his pocket.

Dobel felt sick.

He felt in his pocket. This was his hallucination, after all, although Comfort had thrown some doubt on that point, and therefore he ought to find money in his pocket – yes. He pulled out a handful of shiny silver coins and thrust them at the old sandwich-board man.

The girl and her escort, hawking, left, the words: 'Disgusting!' and 'Shouldn't be allowed!' high and complaining floating after them.

The old man straightened up laboriously, the top board seemingly too heavy for his fragile spine. He saw the silver money in Dobel's hand. His face – what there was visible behind the hair and the alcohol colouring – showed offended dignity.

'I, sir,' he said in that graveyard wheeze, 'am not begging!'

He shuffled off, the boards swaying, the words big and demanding and so easily illegible. A passing car changed gear and blue smoke gushed about him. He coughed again, deep and bell-like, raking around in his stripped lungs for just a few more cells to cough up.

'Silly old fool!' Dobel said after him. 'He doesn't have to do that. He could be in a home – there must be insurance to cover him, assistance, some help – If only he hadn't refused my help!'

Again he had to face the unpalatable fact. His own estimation of himself had been just a little more eroded.

Once again he had been made to feel small.

'We always call him Vincent,' Zack Conrad said to Tony

Lawrence as they turned off Pearl Avenue ready to head back to the Avenue of the Spheres.

'That's his name, isn't it?' Lawrence spoke with a chopping shortness. If they hadn't been Friends he would have been insulting and then Conrad would have had to – and then they'd have fought and then the survivor's Insurance Company would have had to look out for the deceased to strike at them from the grave via his own Insurance Policy. . . . Life would have been intolerable, Conrad pondered in a way he realised dimly had been forced on him by the novel experiences that had befallen him since this search had begun, no wonder Companies stuck together.

'Yes, it's his name,' Conrad said with a new and humble patience. 'But also his names are Arthur Vincent Cheesman. Like us, he has a full roster of names, unlike those filthy worker scum, who are dubbed a name and left to get on with it at the rèche.'

'So?'

'So maybe he signed himself in as Cheesman. I know he dislikes Arthur.'

'He's always been Vincent to me and Vincent he'll remain. Come on, Zack.'

Lawrence had regained his aplomb now he had bypassed the workers.

'I'll tell you this, though, Tony. Vincent is one of the best guys we have left. We just cannot afford to lose him – '

'Lose him?' Lawrence paused in the shadows of a disused garage on the corner of the Avenue. 'You manic?'

'You know what I mean.'

'Don't be obscene.'

Lawrence hated even to think that a man might not recover under the prick of the revivifying needle.

They looked along the avenue under the sinking sun. Soon twilight would make of their search a task too dangerous even for desperate men. Their own emotions were so tightly controlled within themselves, their flippant way of handling emergencies so hidebound, that perhaps they even fooled themselves over the desperate rat-like frenzy that possessed them. Fear they could feel and show over trivia, like being threatened by workers; but over the big threat outlined to them by Sturm, over that, they could only return a blank and icy stare to fate.

Conrad used the scanner. Infra-red showed nothing unusual.
'One more sign,' he said hopefully.

'There it is.' Lawrence pointed.

Yellow and purple lamps coiled upwards never-endingly and white star-bursts picked out the emerald fire above.

THE ONE AND ONLY
LAKE O' FIRE DRAMA DREAMLAND
Clean couches
ALL LUCIMECHS EXPERTLY RECONDITIONED
No waiting

'I see it.' Conrad started walking. 'Vincent never did use a lucimech, did he?'

'Not that I know of. Mind you, I don't know him all that well. A man of mystery, the great AVC, always was, I say.'

'A big man, though. If he's on a trip it won't be too bad. If we find him.'

'If.'

'Drawing a fellow out of a lucimech landscape really takes some doing – so Sturm was saying.'

Lawrence wasn't having that. 'Yes. Sturm told me once they drained the juice out of a girl so deep she wouldn't be fit to take a landscape in three weeks – '

'She was dry all that time?'

The horror of that swamped Conrad's resentment at Lawrence's clumsy attempt to outplay him.

'Yes. She went manic, of course; but they pulled her around with a cyclopropan.'

'I don't know what we'd do without those old three dimensional geometry molecules. Drugs just wouldn't be the same.' Conrad stepped around fallen brickwork. 'But it's a real pan-colour all-glitter horrorshow, though.'

'Yes. Sturm said the recharge jolt was the biggest lift he's ever had – '

'He took it himself? But, of course, he would – '

'You don't get to be Insurer without some privileges accruing.'

Conrad fingered his own Company badge. 'Yes,' he said, feeling the needlework and the electronics. 'Yes.'

They approached the Lake o' Fire.

The building housing it puzzled Conrad at first and then

with an amused contempt, he saw the building had once been a Worker's Library.

A few chipped and tattered painted signs still hung crookedly from the first floor windows. He put his head on one side and then the other to read them. They were all about, as far as he could determine, the joys of reading books, of listening to tapes, of watching films. They made him smile a little. He enjoyed a good book, he would fight anyone who denied that. But of what use could books be to workers? The work they did – poor deluded fools! – had been thrust into them in hypnotic sessions. Books and tapes and culture on any level was wasted on workers. There could be no argument about that.

Why, wasn't *Tom's Garland* required reading at the earliest levels of the Uppers' schools – and surely that carried sufficient authority to convince the meanest of minds that workers were honourable scum, deluded into believing they shared in the general prosperity and were entitled to a garland to steel and gold – poor fools!

Lawrence saw what the place had been and sniggered.

'A good trip or an inscape on a lucimech will do a worker more good than a whole shelf-full of books.' His mind, too, naturally ran on the Hopkins lines. 'Keep them in their place – it's a pity we have to suffer them at all.'

'Noblesse oblige,' Conrad said, cynicism caried as far as it would go. Over workers no Upper had a conscience. 'I feel like a jolt of joy juice right now.'

'Don't we all,' said Lawrence. 'If those workers we saw came on to here – '

Conrad shook his head as much for his own self-satisfaction as to reassure Lawrence. 'No. Shouldn't think so. They were heading for that factory. For sure.'

No one moved about this benighted city without the strongest and most unbreakable of reasons. Workers moved to factories and offices, workers went to tripjoints for the reality that meant more than reality itself. Uppers collected the drained juice for their own use. Sometimes, ever more rarely as they were killed off, loners wandered the city streets, crazed and filthy and begging. No one ventured into the city without being forced.

No one did anything that deprived them of their couch and their trip or their lucimech unless overpowering reasons forced

51

them – if the workers did not report in to their factories they did not receive their entitlement of trips. Nothing at all could be a stronger motive than that – nothing. There were no overpowering reasons.

The Lake o' Fire was laid out in similar lines to those of Aladdin's Cave. Conrad and Lawrence moved quickly and fastidiously among the racked oblivious lumps of quasi-humanity. Distaste as much as fear drove them to hurry.

They found no trace of Arthur Vincent Cheesman.

'I didn't think we would.' Lawrence, as they came out, brisked with purpose. The sun had almost set, and with the shadows' lengthened grip a chill sidled over the city stones. 'He never came down here. Maybe the others had better luck at their end.'

'I hope so.' Conrad rubbed his hands together, looking with apprehension over the purpling shadows. The avenue looked like a wedge of teethmarks, hard and sharp. Once, a long time ago now, at this hour the avenue would have been filled with people, rushing helter-skelter about all the busy details of their lives. That was before the age of Material Plenty had blown up. Before the Uppers had rerigged the balance of society to their own advantage: rather, until they had increased the imbalance that had been fixed from the time the first man beat another to hunt his meat for him.

The air above their heads between the monoliths would have been alive with the thrum of fliers and helitaxis, the pedways and speedways thronged with men and women seeking the open joys of entertainment, sloughing off the weariness of the day's toil, the pavements and walkways crowded as the citizens moved in that seemingly-eternal tide-motion in cities around the glode.

All that busy movement was hopelessly old-fashioned now. A cautionary symbol of the errors into which those old folk had fallen. Nowadays everyone lay on couches to take a trip. That, everyone knew complacently, was far more civilized.

'I feel so exposed out here,' grumbled Lawrence, looking up the Avenue of Spheres. 'When is the saga'd thing coming?'

'I called out as soon as we found nothing.' Conrad looked with unease along the avenue where no friendly lights shone in golden garlands along the boulevards.

'There he is!' Lawrence's voice broke with relief.

The car slid up to them with a whining grumble from an engine unused to exercise. The front wheels hit the kerb clumsily and bounced back. Dirk Havergen looked out of the window, his plump face sweating, his lips petulant with worry. His hands held the steering wheel with a death grip.

'Get in quickly, Friends,' he said, operating the rear door mechanism. Conrad and Lawrence jumped in.

'Trouble, Dirk?'

'Not yet. We were wondering if your radio had gone on the blink – you were a damned long time calling out and we had no idea where you were.'

'If our radio had failed – ' Conrad disliked even thinking of that.

'Knock it off, Dirk!' said Lawrence, pulling his gun out and placing it with delicacy on his knees. The car started off complainingly and headed south towards the upper end of the city.

One tyre was flat and the car lurched in a bounding uneven rhythm; but Havergen's inept handling contributed as much to the car's manner of progress. The flub-flub-flub of the flat tyre got on Conrad's nerves. But he didn't know how to make the tyre good again and he most certainly did not wish to stop the car and start trying to find out. He had heard about the Loopers who prowled the street at night. He didn't know if they really existed or not; but he believed in them.

'What kept you?' asked Havergen, not looking around, his gaze grimly fixed forward through the windscreen. There was no rear view mirror. One was hardly necessary.

'We had to – ah – avoid a gang of workers,' said Lawrence, fondling his gun.

'Sooner you than me.' Havergen, although a Friend and of the same Insurance Company, had built a reputation for casual direct comment. 'I'll bet you were scared.'

'So – ' began Lawrence.

'Like anyone,' Conrad said at the same time. The contra-chiming words flowered and allowed the possible argument to die stillborn.

'If only we knew how long Vincent was going to be away,' said Havergen with frustrated emphasis. 'Sturm thinks we can handle the problem if we begin on it now. Every delay adds to the difficulties.'

The mention of Sturm in connection with obvious platitudes showed Havergen's ineptitude at play.

Lawrence said: 'That is why Sturm asked us personally to search here – the lower end – the dangerous end.'

Havergen moved his shoulders in annoyance and Conrad sneered at him. He was patently no match even for Lawrence at play. Lawrence curled a hand round the butt of his gun and wedged himself more securely back in his seat against the plungings of the car.

Conrad said: 'Is this the only car available, Dirk? Or have you been incapable again of mending the others?'

'Sturm said – ' began Havergen.

'The cars, Dirk, the cars,' said Lawrence, speaking softly.

Havergen's neck shone a ruddy strip between his hair and his yellow shirt collar. Conrad and Lawrence exchanged glances. They didn't like each other; but they liked Havergen less, and this sport pleased them.

'You know as well as I do there are too few cars in the world now. No one knows how to make any more – '

'Not doesn't know how,' said Conrad, correcting. 'Doesn't care to bother. We can get by with what we have left if clods like you would take the necessary trouble to repair them properly.'

'If you weren't in my Insurance – ' Havergen fell back on the standard gambit when losing at play.

'But we are all Friends here,' Lawrence pointed out with animal pleasure. 'So play away, Friends.'

They had good fun driving back home – flub-flub-flub.

At an intersection they saw two dark figures apparently struggling together. Lawrence said: 'Stop! This could be better fun!' He lifted his gun as the car halted.

5

The rest of the shift passed in a vague turmoil of impressions, and Sheldon, with many long puzzled looks through the plate-glass at Minch, struggled to keep the economy going. Everything he did, everything any of them performed in the factory had as its sole aim the simple continuation of the economy as it was. They provided the fuel for the nuclear piles, they coded out the mining computers, they authorised manufacturing industries to continue manufacturing, they saw to it that people, workers and those Others, continued to live in comfort – no: his mind must be wandering. They did not live in comfort. People lived.

People lived for the trips.

He relished the colours in his head. His last trip still bothered him. But he would soon be back on the couch and delving once more into his own beauty-haunted dreamworld, an euphoric ecstasy of colour whorls, haunted with the fragrance of half-forgotten delights.

Then he remembered that this shift he was due for a session in the gym and he made a face as he pressed the buttons controlling steel and textiles and drugs.

Damn the gym!

After a full shift a man wanted to gobble his food down in the canteen and then rush back to the pad and flop out on the couch. The next shift came around again all too soon.

'If only,' Sheldon said as millions had said, 'If only I didn't have to work! If only I could spend all my life dreaming on my couch! Be-yoo-tiful!'

But those Others, the Uppers, insisted. 'No,' they said with

55

their supercilious tones. 'You must work. No workee, no eatee. See?'

Sheldon, like everyone else, saw.

Minch made a face at him through the plateglass.

The surprise of that did not hit him with the force it would have done before he'd tended her wounded temple. He made a face back, and . . .

. . . Arms and legs, rounded and smooth, cleaving blue seas, splashing into foam the tropic sunshine-loaded waves, frangipani in her hair, so dark and lustrous, floating on the water like an intimate cloud. . . .

She flung herself away from her side of the plateglass. Sheldon felt his cheeks burning. Damn these nudisms! They struck with a shrewdness he could neither understand nor explain.

As soon as the shift bells rang he ran out of his console cubicle, anxious to have done with the nonsense in the gym. Minch, dragging her left foot after her, halted him in the corridor. Plateglass lined each side of that boxed-in-tunnel, reflecting them grotesquely.

'Thanks for – you know – Sheldon – '

'I don't know why I did it. Anyway, I'm due in the gym. Coming?'

She shook her head. 'I'm excused fifty per cent of gym period.'

'Why? No one else of my clique is – have you got a special arrangement?' he demanded with sudden fierce suspicion.

'Silly – no – no one can escape the obligations of their duty without very good cause. She touched her leg with a finger tip.

'I don't know whether to believe you or not.' Sheldon still felt suspicious.

The man with the sunken face passed them, hunching himself to himself, not looking at them, about his own business – which was as it should be. A few other workers moved slowly on to shift or with eager alacrity off.

'I'm wasting time talking to you.' Sheldon began to walk briskly for the stairs.

'Wait for me – '

He looked back at her, seeing again that rounded leg bent and hobbling. 'Why? Anyway, what do you keep bending your leg like that for? It looks a perfectly good leg to me.'

She smiled. So that smile was only a pasted grimace; but it was a grimace she had learned – painfully – over the years of her life. 'It is – except that it won't do what legs should do. Go on to the gym, Sheldon.'

'I am.' He moved on and then, perhaps with the uneasy feeling of the nudisms still pervading his body, he halted. He didn't know why. But he said: 'Will you be on the same time tomorrow?'

'Yes.'

'Oh?' He didn't know what to say next. 'Really?'

He walked away, holding his back upright.

Central Welfare took care of the workers.

Central Welfare made sure they looked after themselves.

Central Welfare told them *when* and *how* and *who* – but never, ever, *why*.

Sheldon walked into the organised noise and drumfire of the gym feeling, as always, a wrenching back of his mind to his days in the crèche. He could remember those days with reasonable clarity, though the clashing coloured symbols and dreams remembered from his trips; and always for a reason he could not comprehend, they saddened him.

Everyone could remember back to the crèche, where they'd learned to walk and to talk, mixing in with the other kids, being trained up to their duties as factory or office workers, organised to handle the destinies of the nation. They formed their own cliques, of course, as soon as they were allowed to go on trips.

He'd heard latrine whispers that things were not arranged thus with the Uppers; but then the Uppers did no work and thus were debarred from the real man's world that led to the even more real world of trips and lucimechs.

He started in on the parallel bars and then went to punching a bag. Like everyone else, he toned up quite naked, his red smock hung on a numbered hook. If he forgot the number it didn't matter; any old smock would do.

Girls and some older women, boys and men, all together, all naked, all exercising with a single frantic haste to get their prescribed sequence of contortions over with and get the hell out of here back to their couches. The gym spat noises at the glass roof. Like a dry aquarium the gym displayed the white bodies, the black bodies, the brown and red and yellow bodies, of human beings as though they were fish, gape mouthed and disc-eyed, behind unfeeling glass.

When the dingg-dongg-dingg of the letting-out bell chimed across the writhing bedlam, the rush to the smocks, led by the fleetest and lost by the weakest knocked down by sturdier bodies, found Sheldon well out in front, chest heaving with victory, as he burst from the factory into the dusk-blued streets.

Like shrapnel the workers radiated out from the factory seeking their pads, or tripjoints or lucimech palaces.

Sheldon pulled on his cape that he had had time only to sling across his shoulder. In one of its pockets his knife lay snugged in sheath, a ready friend in case a non-clique worker asked the wrong questions. Workers tended to avoid each other, intent on their couches. But sometimes – sometimes – Sheldon had killed his man and had half-forgotten in the clamour of his colours.

He hadn't bothered to eat at the canteen because of the delay imposed on him by the gym period and he wondered with little mental reality if Deedee would have anything hot. If she had a cut of cold meat he would probably miss out and hit the couch at once. The thought of sitting at table and eating when the couch and the needle glared at him from the other side of the pad struck him as a fine example of the waste in material things they were often warned against. Waste – who the hell worried about waste? Get the old needle stuck in, get the old lucimech whirling, let waste worry about itself – ha!

He almost bumped into Minch standing beneath the dappled shadow of a fallen arch of the monorail.

Two stub arms of arch reached out and over, curving in mute desire for each other, eternally separated where the keystone had fallen.

'I wanted to see you, Sheldon,' she spoke urgently, breathily, frightened.

'Get lost!' he said, pushing past.

'But Sheldon – I – my clique – I knew it would happen one day – Sheldon, I want you to let me join your clique.'

'Do what?' He scarcely heard her, the noises of his colours resounding in his head. 'Buzz off, Minch. I've got to get to my pad.'

'Take me with you! Please, Sheldon –'

'Don't bother me. I'll hit you if you keep on.'

58

'I know it's not usual to change cliques late like this – I'm eighteen, you know – but Garstang threw me out after I fell down – that is – Sheldon, you will take me, won't you?'

Something of what she was saying penetrated. Join the clique! That would take some discussion, if that could be arranged, it was always difficult. Griselda might welcome a new girl; she'd been happy when Deedee joined. But the men, Francis and Sammy, both taciturn and tough, might object. There were too many damn girls in the clique already, flopping about on their couches, taking everything and unable to fight properly if the clique was invaded.

'No, Minch,' he said impatiently. 'No go. Buzz off.'

'I can shoot a gun! I can! *Please*, Sheldon.'

'Have you got any rations?'

'Yes, yes. And my own needle. I'm paid up to date in a Funeral Club.'

'What a stinking waste that is! Let the city bury you like they bear you.'

She responded to the argument, seeing her plea half won.

'All right, anything! Only please let me come with you.' Her heavy mass of hair fell forward over her face as she said, faintly: 'I'm scared of the Loopers!'

'Them!'

'They do exist, Sheldon, I'm sure they do!'

'Old women's stories.' He felt around with his hand until he could touch his knife in its sheath in his cloak. 'Frightening kids.'

'And,' she said in a pathetic effort to clinch the plea, 'I haven't any rations, only my needle, my clique kept them all, and I'm without money for a tripjoint –'

'So you're going dry in an hour or so?'

'Yes, Sheldon!' she clutched at his arm. 'Oh, yes!'

Much as he disliked everyone except the members of his own clique – and some of them he was not overfond of – he found something odd about even thinking about this girl as a human being of his clique when she was not. If she joined then at least that dichotomy would be resolved. He could think clearly, sometimes, even if he could never articulate those thoughts with clarity.

'Well – ' he said.

'Sheldon,' she said, and . . .

... A white netsuke of flesh, they formed a rounded single entity, her softness and his hardness twinned and one, red pouting lips and her violet eyes so close, so close, her hair massy and perfumed and threaded with golden roses and silver lilies, entwining his strength. . . .

'Get away!' he gasped.

She recoiled, staggering, arms upraised blindly.

He jumped towards her, seized her violet smock beneath her cape, shook her. 'What do you want with me? Why do you pester me – why, why, why?'

Her head lolled as he shook her.

'Sheldon – you're – you're hurting me – '

He didn't know it and he couldn't feel where. He gripped her like a rag doll, ready to thrust her away from him. He heard her gasp, saw her eyes roll.

'You – help – no one else – '

Clasped in his arms with an embrace of anger, she began to scream.

'I'm tired, Tony,' Conrad said boredly.

Havergen, perhaps to ease out of the one-sided play, stopped the car. He said drawlingly: 'Sturm approves this kind of play more than – '

'I know,' Lawrence said. His mouth drew together and the left corner kept rising in an irritating tic. 'You just keep quiet and leave this to the men.'

Conrad wanted a jolt of joy juice. Lawrence, it seemed, had had a fix later than he. 'Hurry it up, Tony. I'm dry.'

'Hard luck, Friend,' said Havergen, daring.

Lawrence squeezed his hand on the gun butt until the skin and walnut shrieked. He smiled. He smiled! He opened the door and got out, swinging his legs briskly, holding his shoulders back to display his badge. His pale blue shirt and slacks merged with the evening dusk, a wraith among wraiths.

Feeling irritable and dry and very cross, Conrad got out as well. 'You stay here,' he told Havergen bluntly.

Seeing a large group of workers and hiding from them in daylight was a very different proposition from dealing with a twosome in the evening. Even Conrad saw the sense in that.

The best line he could take was doing what he was doing;

let Lawrence get it over with and then try to hurry the man back home.

They were very much two Uppers as they approached the two workers.

Conrad walked half a pace behind Lawrence. He kept his hand down near his own gun butt, just in case Lawrence fouled things up, or became too squeamish, although the latter suggestion scarcely merited consideration.

He could see now that the couple seemed to be arguing, a man and a woman, arguing here in the shadows of the shattered monorail. The oddness of that had just begun to surprise him, when . . .

. . . The girl and he, alone, supported on strands of nylon, swaying beneath a glass dome, the suns of all space shining through, the girl's face hidden from him by dark and massy hair, heavy with promise, and all about them the shining space of light and colour and song, blossoming. . . .

Conrad jerked back, his face distorted, his hands shaking. The girl swung around to face him, her hair swirling to conceal her features so that all he could see was a rippling dark fall of hair. Lawrence halted, surprised by the sudden movement.

The man with the girl lifted his right hand and threw.

Lawrence, his gun snouting evilly to enforce his will, his face half-turned away from Conrad, said slickly: 'I want to show you a game – ' He stopped saying those exact and precisely enunciated words. Instead, he said: 'Ugh-g-g-g-glumph!' He dropped his gun. His knees buckled. He put his hands up to his chest but he could not quite reach the hilt of the knife protruding between his ribs. Blood ran out and down his light blue shirt.

His pretty badge sucked up the blood greedily.

Tony Lawrence fell down on to his knees, bent over, holding himself. Slowly – so slowly – he bent forward farther and farther until his head touched the ground. Then he rolled slowly sideways. His legs kicked once or twice. He said: 'K-k-k-k – ' and so died.

Already his badge, monitoring heart and respiration and temperature and the sudden kicking release of adrenalin, would be transmitting the information to Insurance House. There the incoming signals would be in the process of being picked up, assigned a source, and direction finders would even now be pin-pointing the place of death. Within minutes the Insurance Adjusters would be on their way.

Conrad stood there stupidly. None of that mattered to Lawrence. Lawrence was dead. All the science in this world wouldn't bring him to life again.

Looking up and quite without thought that another knife might streak towards him, Conrad could not see the worker or the girl.

They had vanished into the night.

Conrad felt sick. His legs trembled. He bent down reluctantly and looked at Lawrence's face. On that mask of pleasure the last moments of life had stamped an awful knowledge. Lawrence, ready to enjoy himself, had instead taken the last long trip of all.

'What – what?'

'Run, you fool girl, *run*!'

'I can't – I can't – my leg!'

'Your damned leg – here – '

'Oh – don't drop me!'

'Hold on, then. I don't know why I'm bothering with you.'

'It's so dark – '

'The darker the better! Now shut your yap! I've got to get us both out of this – '

'But that man – that Upper! – you killed him!'

'What else?'

'But – '

'Wrap up Minch, or I'll drop you.'

Silence.

Sheldon took more than his usual care this night in ensuring the run in to the pad was unobserved. Each clique carefully preserved the location of its pad in the decaying and abandoned builldings of the city. Raids were not uncommon and invariably produced bitter recriminations. Not every worker worked. A fix was a fix whether it came from Central Welfare or from the stolen hoard of a raided clique.

Like a slinking cat he crept through the derelict lower stories of the apartment block, dragging Minch along by one thin wrist, cursing her beneath his breath for dragging one leg.

'Now you know whereabouts our location is at, Minch, if

anything happens – I'll have to kill you. You see that, I'm sure.'

'Yes, Sheldon,' she said. That was a common-sense precaution she understood. Understanding, in this case, did not lessen her fear.

The cumbered stairs of the building, whose treads of concrete gapped yellow and brown, fell below them as at each carefully casually arranged block Sheldon passed through and then adjusted the encumbrance. It might be a heap of fallen masonry; an abandoned perambulator, a baby-carriage that nevermore would carry babies who now thrived at the crèches; planks artfully angled to collapse at an incautious thrust; refuse of every sort. The wires and strings that rang the alarm bells were more carefully disguised lest by their very presence they betrayed what they were designed to conceal.

Sheldon, whose throat now resembled the dry plaster of the bare walls, pushed through the door into the pad and made very sure that he stood in front of Minch, holding her behind him close, clinging, hearing her gasping panting. Griselda half-pushed up from her couch, her big soft body like a pregnant hippopotamus, then slacked back with a sigh. Francis and Sammy had both gone, their beds now being occupied by Big Sack and Duboys, both far gone on a trip. Chloe and Doris were in the act of being shaken awake by Patti, who looked nearly as dry as Sheldon. Her straggly orange hair had been screwed into a bun and she still wore her cape. She worked at a different factory from Sheldon and thus her smock had originally been of a bright blue colour, now stained and faded into a pale document of toil.

'Hurry them two she-cats up, Patti,' Thomasina was saying from the shelf. In her thin hands the needle showed sharp and clean. Her face, gaunt and pinched like Patti's, showed an intense, concentrating, adoring wisdom as she filled the needle.

Both women looked up as Sheldon entered. Their faces betrayed no interest whatsoever. They both went back to what they were doing. Then the presence of Minch obtruded itself like a dreamform in a trip, demanding an attention they had no wish to spare.

'Who's she, then?' asked Patti, clouting Chloe around the head. 'Wake up, you skinny ratbag!'

'She's Minch,' said Sheldon. Then, before he could stop

himself, he said: 'She's joining the clique.'

'Oh, yes? What'll Big Sack say? Hey?'

'It'll be all right. Hurry up and get those two cows back to work and hit your fix. I'm dry!'

'What's it look like I'm trying to do, stoopid?' demanded Patti truculently. She slapped Chloe again, let her go to strike at Doris, and Chloe immediately fell back on to the wrinkled sheets.

'Have you stuck 'em with the old Horrible Truth?'

'Of course, idiot! They'd never even be awake if I hadn't done that.'

Sheldon hated any interruption when he returned from shift with only the couch and the trip ahead. Anybody did, it stood to reason. Minch clung to him, a sick and silly smile half on her face.

'Well give 'em another jab.' If a revivifying needle failed to work properly at first time, what else should you do? 'Give it to 'em again,' he said savagely.

Chloe snorted and flung her arms around, then, as though moving through molasses, she moaned and sat up, creaking.

'Oh my saga'd back!' she said. 'Is this the Horrible Truth?'

'Yes,' said Patti. 'And you're on my couch stopping me from taking a trip. Get orf of it, you fat cow!'

Thomasina came over and between her and Patti they pushed Chlore and Doris on to the floor.

'They're worse than kids starting on playing the mouth organ,' said Thomasina disgustedly.

Sheldon knew that the off duty pair would hit their fix right now and wouldn't worry their heads about Chloe and Doris who should be at work. If these two didn't earn their money to buy their drugs or spend in a tripjoint or to buy food – well, then, they just wouldn't. Maybe once they'd be allowed to freeload on the rest of the clique – that was one reason for cliques to exist – but Big Sack wouldn't let anyone – anyone – freeload on him.

'Get up and go to work,' said Sheldon, kicking Chloe with a prodding toe. He let the same action kick off his slipper and with a second kick rid himself of the other. 'Where's your needle?' he said to Minch, pulling her around and in front of him. She trailed her leg and hopped a couple of times to keep up with the speed of his pull.

'Here,' she said with a gasp, holding her side. She took her case from a cape pocket.

'On that shelf.' Sheldon nodded. 'No couch for you. All occupied. Deedee will be in soon for that one. On the floor.'

All the time he spoke he had been taking down his own needle and filling it with reality.

He lay down. Sure, he was hungry. But that could wait. He didn't bother to see what Chloe and Doris did. He didn't care what Minch did. He wanted just one thing. His colours beckoned to him. The feel of reality waved enticingly before him.

The world around him meant less than a grain of sand beneath his foot.

Only the reality of the life that expanded before him now like a vast and scented flower, opening out, engulfing him and drawing him in, head and chest and arms and legs, going, going, going. . . .

He was away on a trip and life was real at last.

6

The man who had decided in a casual moment of boredom to call himself Wendell, and then Higham, and then Dobel, experimenting with the semantic nuances of words and names within the context of hallucinations, had by now realised something was wrong.

Standing in the last stages of evening in the hallucinatory carbon-monoxide-poisoned and traffic-deafening mid-twentieth-century city, he hesitated, worried.

He did not intend to stay here. He must change his name again. But there lay the danger. To what name should he shift? Any name brought peril. To choose the wrong name would be comimitting suicide.

Unused to bustling traffic and hurrying people, Dobel, as perforce he was for now, felt a sharp shoulder nudge him ungently. He staggered. His foot slipped on the greasy kerb, jarred off, unbalanced him and sent him pitching into the street. He heard a woman scream. He heard a high and snake-like hissing. He heard a locked shrieking of brakes. With frantic eyes he saw a shining square grilled mouth bearing down on him. His bulging eyes watched in total horror as the mass plunged towards him.

Instantly, with no other choice, he decided he would call himself Commer.

He lay uncomfortably on his side, staring through a window with frames of green and yellow and red, harshly coloured. Buildings, white-faced and pock-marked with windows, crowded helplessly together. A paratrooper floated down towards a head-on clash where a blue-faced man, moronic and sardonic, taunted a transformation of Bast, cat-bodied, human-

66

headed, a yellow-furred inversion. Flowers grew into a crown and beyond the background shifting planes of colour, dimensions of light and silent sounds clashed and interpenetrated. The tower stood, palsied by searchlights, would-be arrogant and lace-like in insubstantiality.

Out of sight unending rows of white crosses covered acres of ground.

Commer stood up, disturbed and uneasy. He took a single step forward and the man with the blue face, who now, Commer saw, wore a black mask, turned his head, saying: 'If you take the Verdun line you may never win through – or you may. I have no mercy on you.'

When he resumed his pose Commer saw that he was really Janus, and he knew, then, that his journey had begun.

Commer swung about to see a nude woman with three eyes perpendicularly one above the other in place of a face float past, her coffin following her on fat pneumatic wheels. He felt the sickness of coldness and decay. When, he wondered with growing despair, would he descend to that eye-walled subterranean lagoon of sapphire and emerald and chrysoprase? When would that corpse-faced witch with shelled skin and finned clothes beckon him with an ancient ritual he could never disobey?

Crabs and cuttlefish and dank-eyed monsters from some skulled hell floated past him, dull and nipping and bearded with slime.

Commer said, firmly and aloud: 'I am called Smith.'

Silence.

Darkness.

Silence and Darkness.

It could break me now, Smith thought. The cold and the wet, the no-noise and the no-light. They could all break me.

His fingers touched a door handle. He knew it was a door handle by the feel of cleaned brass, the roundness and heaviness of it, the comforting feel of the roundness plump in his palm.

He twisted and pushed.

The pounding beat of drums, guitars and electronic organs hit him. Keyed to the plink-plonk beat of the human heart, the backing rhythms plucked him bodily into a vast room, columned, domed, ecstatically lit by brilliant bunches of electric lights. Girls and boys, miniskirted and bare of chest, danced and danced and danced. Colour, light, heat, odours of hamburgers and crisps, of beer and Tizer, of good-humoured reek of living, fulminating furiously, happy.

'Smith,' he said to himself. 'Never go wrong with a name like that.'

There had been nothing wrong, he knew well enough, with the name Commer, or any of the other names. The trouble lay all in the adulterants that had been criminally allowed to defile the pure stuff. He could not now remember for how long he had planned to be on this trip or even if he had programmed Guztav Lawlor's computer to bring him back to that other reality with the revivifying needle – the workers called it the Horrible Truth, he felt with great justification – but when he did not get back he would so berate Lawlor that – hell! He'd get the man's licence revoked, and the Ring would deal with him.

He felt overdressed in shirt and slacks as he edged his way around the dance floor. The music baroomed and zapoweed and stomp-stomp-stomped from speakers set everywhere Couples danced with transistor sets strapped to their arms, oblivious and sent. He had to duck gyrating arms and legs, sidetrack around couples who stood like tree-trunks opposite each other, moving only their feet in tiny delicate paddlings that scarcely disturbed the time stream at all. Everybody, after their fashion, was having a ball.

At the far end of that bedlam of happy confusion he saw a door and the word – in English, thankfully – 'Buffet'. The irony struck him and, murmuring 'Merci, messieurs,' he went through.

The room appeared not quite so crowded and the smells of delectable food appreciably elevated. He found a plate and was about to pile it with sausages and chips when a voice, deep and somehow yearning, said: 'Would you care to pass me a plate of the same, my friend?'

The friend meant anything, here in an hallucination, where Insurance Companies merely insured you against fate and not against your fellow man. If any man other than yourself could be allowed a fellow. The point had never been adequately resolved.

'Certainly,' said Smith. He heaped a second plate and then

turned, holding out both plates like a waiter.

The man who had spoken stood in the corner. His facial appearance – a long sallow face with round eyeglasses and very dark hair brushed back, dignified with silver threads – meant nothing to Smith. Neither did his sartorial elegance – a dark blue suit, hand-sewn, a narrow maroon tie and a white nylon shirt of impeccable fit – mean anything. Smith gaped at the barrel in which the man stood. Its wood shone with a dark and polished patina. Great care in cooperage had gone into the making of that barrel. The iron bands shone with a silver glow.

'I see you like my little barrel.' The man took the plate and began to eat, hungrily but with exquisite fastidiousness, not dropping any crumbs into his barrel.

'Ah – yes,' said Smith, eating also.

'Oh, yes, this is quite the most excellent barrel I've ever had. I used to go through them, you know. Oh, yes, confounded things, always leaking when it rained, or springing a hoop and letting the staves go slack.' He rapped on the barrel and produced a mellow gong note. 'This is a tight cask you see, made by the best wet cooper in the business.'

'It looks – ah – very fine.'

The man smiled most charmingly. 'By the way, my name's really Diogenes, you know. I can have it printed up any time I like. But I prefer to let people call me Gray.'

'You don't seem,' said Smith around a sausage, 'to be very cynical – '

'Yes, I know what you mean. But then, I'm not free from emotion either, you see. I certainly lack shame – hand me another sausage will you, there's a good fellow – and nature holds the answers to all our problems.'

Smith had relaxed. This encounter was following the pattern of his usual hallucinations. To meet interesting people, talk to them, pick out of his own subconscious the crumbs of knowledge hidden all unsuspected there – yes, this made his work valuable and worth while.

'How are you on outworn shibboleths?'

'I'm against them, as I'm against all useless conventions.'

'But are all conventions useless?'

He laughed with gentle concern. 'By no means. Even conventions of horror have many levels of use. I am myself particularly intrigued by horror conventions. Why, if it wasn't for my barrel I would personally go to inspect every horror convention I heard of.'

'Instead of a tub you could use a bath.'

'A bath! Excellent!' The man called Gray whose real name was Diogenes smiled with a flash of teeth and glasses, his lips curving deeply. 'The thought of horror convention in a bath astounds me with fancies too ineffable for mundane lips – ' He went on in that strain for some time. Smith, feeling a sympathetic affection for the logorrhetic, ate his sausages and drank his Tizer.

Choosing Smith had been a wise move. When he got back from this trip he would personally run Guztav Lawlor up to the headquarters of the Ring. If lucimech palace proprietors and tripjoint madams wanted to stay in business they had to join the Ring, and if they violated the principles laid down by the Insurance Companies, then – no lucimech repair and no drugs. Anyone – anyone at all in the world – could be brought to immediate heel by the threat to withdraw drugs or lucimech time.

Anyone.

'Tell me, Smith,' Gray said, indicating with a generous gesture that he required his glass to be filled. 'How are things in your world now?'

'Strange, as ever,' said Smith, obligingly filling Gray's glass. 'The workers still work – thank the light of LSD – and the Uppers still rule and life goes on. Most of the cities are falling down, though, and agriculture is, to phrase it euphemistically, wildly disorganised and declining.'

Gray bit with strong natural teeth into his sausage.

'How do you come by your food, then?'

'Oh, we can still grow and catch enough. There are not many of us, you know. The workers live in their pitiful hidden little clique-houses in crevices in the old collapsing cities, and we Uppers live in vast comfort of body and agonies of mind in the last and most beautiful city sections built. We have all about us the final creations of man's artistic genius. After us, there will be nothing, for we do not produce art.'

'Art,' said Gray, munching. 'It's a value gimmick, that's all. If three people club together and proclaim a cruddy book or a botched picture to be a Great Work of Art and their creators

Great Artists, and these three shout loud enough, they'll find enough fools to believe them.' He chuckled without malice. 'It's happened. In the end Joe Public is served up with rubbish that not only no one can understand but that no one really enjoys. And the big fat slob of a public cooes and cries with joy – just so each one won't be thought of as a fool by his neighbour, who is just as big a fool. Talk about the Emperor's new clothes – that ought to be the critics' new book values.'

'You have a point,' Smith said, half-listening, worrying about why what was happening to him was happening just like this. 'I'm calling myself Smith right now. It's safe. But if I called myself – aha – I won't mention the name – if you don't mind – I could find myself up to the neck and head down in the muck.'

'Tell a good story and grip the public and you can take your critics and put 'em up against a wall for all the good they do.' Gray who was really Diogenes rambled on, eating and drinking with a gusto that created envy among a group of youngsters who walked in, flushed and laughing, from the dance.

'You could be right,' agreed Smith without really hearing. 'In my world there is no art, for no one has time for rubbishy reality, artificially created at second hand. Why read a story or watch a film or listen to music – all at second hand – when you can take a trip and imbibe it all in pan-colour, all-glitter and wondershow? There's no comparison.'

'Don't you want to come back and tell others? Report your findings? Give pleasure to the public? If you did that would be art.'

Smith laughed. This hallucination was making up for the others. His own subconscious was bringing up arguments he had long since discarded – and the relief was so great he could have cried.

'Give pleasure to other people?' he said, chuckling. 'Are you crazy? Who the hell worries about any one else since the days of Material Plenty showed us it was a crime to look out for the other fellow? Help yourself. That's the only rule there is. Why, before the age of Material Plenty men used to give what they called charity. I'm told it was actually a part of their working period – in the token form of money – that they voluntarily parted with to some one else, because they were –

wait for it, it's a laugh! – *sorry* for them!'

'This was wrong?'

'Of course! You can't weaken the economy and weaken your own position by throwing away your own wealth. Let the other fellow look out for himself. It's the only natural way.'

'Didn't they use to say something like: "Love thy neighbour as thyself"?'

'Of course. And it pays. If you're not tough enough to meet the economic and social demands made on you then you'll go under. If you are artificially helped then you're continuing undesirable and non-perpetuating strains of development, falsely keeping in being strains that by their very nature must die eventually.'

'Glib.'

'And true. Look what happened to the human stock when they stopped killing off the diseased and deformed and crippled.'

'But some of those thalidomide people proved of tremendous brain-capacity – wonderful work – '

'That's different.' Smith didn't care, like most people nowadays, which side of an argument he defended just so something in so-called reality happened. 'We weren't keeping in being weak genetic values. If a woman is going to have difficulty in having a baby and will die unless artificially helped, then the law of nature says she should die. You can't stop for a Caesarean if the tribe is migrating and the snows and the wolves are sweeping up the weak and unfit to live – '

'Romantic poppycock,' said Diogenes. 'We live in a civilised community where the wolves have been killed off, central heating is standard, and where a Caesarean can bring happiness to a family – '

'You,' said the man who called himself Smith with a bitterness out of keeping with a happy hallucination, 'are living in the past.'

'As perhaps the last and certainly the greatest art collector the world has ever seen,' said Sturm, leaning back in his leather chair and toying with a Florentine gilt cup, blazing with jewels, 'I feel a sense of mission. A destiny to embody everything we of Earth can show of taste and beauty and true art, and preserve it, so that if in the far future other men come to find what they can of us, they will stand amazed at what was accomplished so long ago.'

Much of what he said could be seen in the hall to be incontrovertibly true. Built long ago as a permanent palatial chamber, so long private electric trolleys had to be used, so wide a shuttle service had been introduced when the electrics began to give out, so high a complete weather cycle took place beneath the roof, rain, cloud, all under the spans since the ancient weather control equipment had broken down, the hall's function had been long forgotten. It existed as one of the largest buildings ever built by the hand of man. Perhaps it had, as some said, been built to hold the chemically-fuelled spaceships built to travel to Mars; built and never even fired off Earth.

Every square inch of the interior surface available between the tall futuristic arrowslits of windows had been covered by canvases. Paintings of every age and every type – even a few Tachiste and incredibly dull Op and Pop art frames, hard edge and tiny, brilliantly dotty Franticidal paintings were represented – covered every surface and hung suspended on laces of aluminium wire, anodised, swinging gently in three-dimensional mobiles of expression.

Sculptures stood everywhere. The three-dimensional space of the vast hangar had been crammed and filled and interpenetrated with articles of art and culture of every description.

En masse the whole effect was one of a chiaroscuro of detail, a single flame-like jewel whose components could not be individually identified. Weather within the building had already attacked some of the earlier paintings, a few violins had lost their silver tones; but within the care concepts of Sturm's people, everything to preserve the giant collection had been done. It held treasures from the Louvre, from the Hermitage, from the Tate, each individual demand for particular care being met by isolating temperature and humidity controls within plastic cells. To climb the spiral staircases between treasures, to walk the flying gangways past art that had flowered thousands of years ago, that had been lost and rediscovered perhaps three or four times in its lifetime, to stand and gaze, picking out well-loved beauties with his portable telescope, these were the joys for Sturm.

These, and women, and the joy juice.

Now and again he would just sit in his real leather chair made for some long gone President and brood, twirling some trifle of unconsidered fortune between his thick fingers. The world, he could see more clearly than most, was finished. The workers were held to their production by tricks, by shams, their numbers every year decreasing. Once a supply of joy juice could not be found from the workers, then the Uppers themselves must contribute it.

Whatever grumbles and curses might be flung at him, whatever puny actions his would-be peers might take, he, Adolf Eric Sturm, would ensure his supply of joy kicks and hell take anyone else.

He had fought his way to Insurer of the Company he had called the Sturm Insurance Company the moment he had taken over. He might have troubles with one or other of the companies in this city but, in the end, he knew with a confidence that rose thickly around him, he would win.

Now he could growl out his challenge against the fall of darkness. He was the greatest art collector the world had ever seen. And, when he went down, the world went down with him.

One of the ring of TV screens lit and Archbold's thin and worried face looked out.

'Sturm? There's no trace of anyone here. We've picked Tony Lawrence up; but – '

'Of course you picked him up.' Sturm controlled the fire in him. 'But what's this nonsense about no one being there?'

'Only Zack Conrad and Dirk Havergen.'

Sturm was prepared to meet this internecine trouble if and when it came. 'Did one of them do it?'

'No. It's quite clear. Worker knife. Conrad handled it, though – '

'The fool!'

'Yes. No trace of the killer.'

Sturm brooded. All this trouble because Vincent had gone off on a bender again. If Vincent wasn't so all-fired important, he would have been dispensed with, long since.

'You'd better keep looking. No knowing what you'll find.' Sturm leant forward, his squat, square, high-boned face suddenly ugly, the thick short-cropped black hair gleaming like a host of spears. 'Turn over a few clique rat-holes. Shake them up. Make them know we're around.'

'If you say so, Sturm.'

'I do say so and don't you forget it.'

Sturm had no need to raise his voice. The icy-grey of his eyes, a madman's eyes, men used to say in the days when he killed them on his way up the ladder, drilled into the marrow of a man's bones, moulding him to Sturm's will. His short, square, massively powerful body, clad always in brown shirt and pants with a leather belt four inches thick, lumbered about on square elephantine legs. His muscles dented like chrome steel. His fists could smash oak.

A great squat barrel of a tank was Adolf Eric Sturm.

The really frightening thing about him was that most of him was real. Most of him was human being. Most of what he was now had grown from the baby born from his mother's womb. Only one eye, part of his intestinal tract, a few bones here and there had been manufactured from plastic and miracle artificial materials. He had not called heavily on the surgeons and their artificial organs. As a matter of the highest priority – far more important than automobiles or aeroplanes or space research or nuclear power – the continuing in being of a body of informed knowledge and expert surgeons simply for the prolongation of human life had seemed to the Uppers a natural object of sensible life. Artificial organs – what the ancients used to call artiforgs – could still be produced and inserted with full operational safety in this culture of decaying technical accomplishment.

Men like Sturm meant to ensure that this state of affairs continued. Look after Number One meant you used your reasoning powers as well as your basic instincts. Sturm could always take a ship across an ocean if he had to go and there were no aircraft left; but he couldn't use anything else other than an artificially implanted liver if his own refused to function. But right now Sturm knew where insurance for the future in personal insurance lay. In the prolongation of life, in the prolifes, lay a single chance for the future of humanity and the postponement of the eventual destiny of his great collection of Human Art.

Another screen lit and Zack Conrad's face looked out with a

tired and old expression that made Sturm think seriously about the boy's future.

'You've made a fine mess of it, Bung!' said Sturm with studied friendly offensiveness.

He was about the only man – certainly the only man in his Insurance Company and possibly in the city – who could combine an insult with the salutation 'Bung', the nearest a citizen could get to a genuinely friendly greeting.

He lolled back in his seat. His office had been sited in a corner of the hangar halfway between floor and ceiling. The glass-walled suite of rooms protruded from the original four-square walls like an insect's nest from a tree cranny, a complex of rooms and apartments as large as a moderately-sized hotel. From it Sturm controlled his empire.

'Tony Lawrence was killed – '

'Yes. That's an extra little blot on the account. Well, cough it up, man!'

'No,' Conrad said, jerking and spluttering over the words. 'We didn't find him. Did anyone else – ?'

'No, of course no one else did.' Sturm, in rapidly approaching the time when he would lose his temper, knew too that he must envision his acts at that time and plan accordingly. 'Universal failure. I do not like failure.'

Sturm's enormous ribcage swelled as he breathed in, the brown shirt like a second skin over muscles that ridged like armour-plating. His square face with the stiff black bristles of hair glowered, downdrawn and vengeful, darkly domineering. 'You will go out again tomorrow, Zack. You will take Dirk Havergen. You will look for Vincent. You will find him. Is that clear?'

Not a syllable over-accented. Not an extra hiss in any aspirate. Not a savage click of consonants. Not a molecule of overt threat. Yet Zack Conrad blinked and swallowed and stuttered over his abject agreement.

Sturm switched off the screen and stood up, automatically flexing his muscles, letting his pectorialis major fight his latissimus dorsi, eventually shrugging everything back into place. He was feeling a little dry, at that.

If they didn't find Vincent soon real trouble could start. There were other biochemists, and other psychiatrists, and other self-styled professors of hallucinology; there were other drugs and mechanics for lucimechs; but there was only one Arthur Vincent Cheesman. 'More's the pity!' finished Sturm, his thoughts as usual breaking out into vocal speech. He didn't care a jot for anyone else, least of all for Vincent; but the fellow had to be found or the structure of worker had hallucinatory production of joy juice would break down.

Life for any Upper without joy juice – Sturm deliberately did not finish off the thought. He had been thinking too much. He craved action. Outside this giant room there was nothing he needed; anything he wanted would be brought here. He took the elevator down four transparent floors to his private gym and knocked hell out of the apparatus for an hour. Sweating lightly he sauntered through the steam bath and the hot rooms, the cold plunge and the roll in the snow. Glowing and primed for devilry, he took the elevator up to his harem.

7

He was away.

He slid between the colours of the spectrum.

Down a long and transparently beautiful slope he 'wheeed!' and 'zoweed!' among glinting glass crystals, among pyrotechnic palettes, among the gleaming arms of women uplifted like the fronds of undersea dream caverns.

Sheldon began his trip with little luggage apart from appetite.

Somewhere for beneath the sea in meridian caves dappled with the eyes of starfish he met a man in a silver cape who waved a wand and said soulfully: 'You are doomed, little man, doomed.' The restless surge of the sea sucked an echoing cry back: 'Doomed – oomed – oomed. . . . '

He finned fast and fervently away with streaks of indigo and gold carolling past him and singing old songs. The water turned into a shower of cold silver coins from a forgotten museum; cold and old and worn. They stung as they scattered past, stung like a myriad of maddened hornets, stung like truth.

Silver coins, hurting, stinging, forgetting.

. She was beautiful. Green hair waved above her head like a tinted sea shell. Her draperies clung to her figure, sculpted, fluted. She floated towards him with her arms outstretched and she trailed her left leg among the trailing gauze. Like a sea wraith she finned towards him from the blue undersea shadows breaking down the cold metal barrier of the silver coins, bringing colour and life and radiance and love.

He held out his arms in longing.

With the smile of a dying nun she passed him by. He watched her go, watched every curve of her body subtly revealed by the turquoise mesh. She moved past him like a mist dissipating at dawn.

A crash of symbols unheard and unwanted left him.

A placard screeched at him. Something about the Right to Strike against the Law is the inalienable right of the worker left him. She had left him. He tried to follow, tried to seek her out, tried to catch a vanishing glimpse of that turquoise mesh of allurement.

Her face and figure left him.

He was left, he saw as he turned about slowly and with terror, alone and bereft on a dusty plain where bleached bones and unknown artifacts beneath an open excoriated sky proclaimed the universal end of everything.

'No!' he screamed, lifting his arms high in a gesture of pleading forgotten for a thousand years. 'No! Bring her back –' But he did not really mean bring back the girl in the turquoise mesh; he meant bring back something he did not know he had lost, something for which he could only cry like a child asking for the boon of old age.

How long after that he wandered, alone and desolate through desert after desert, crawling through the vasty eye sockets of gigantic skulls, he did not know. When at last he reached the white road and crept up it against a roaring unheard wind and saw across the lake the island and its reflection forming a leering mouth of horror he gave way to final defeat, letting the wind blow him back where it willed. . . .

At the southern end of the city between the old solid open-planned endoskeletal building and the cloud coping vastness of Sturm's room, the Uppers' city rose, a covered-over fairy-land of exoskeleton buildings. Between two solid chunks of rooted masonry had been sited the greatest concentration of mobile architecture. The idea of exoskeletal buildings had been ages old when the Uppers' city had been built, and they had at first played laughingly with their tractive rooms, changing positions at whim, uncoupling and coupling service lines, water, electricity, food, refuse, canned entertainment. The world had been young at heart, then, on the verge of everything that had lain in promise over the centuries since that first hesitant step up with the lever and the wheel and fire.

Mankind had been on the verge of so much – telepathy, a

sound and happy economy caring for everyone, happiness for all, the banishment of disease, the opening-up of the solar system and, eventually, the stars. Everything had been in the balance, the promise so great and so tremblingly near fulfilment.

Then the Uppers discovered Joy Juice.

And the Age of Material Plenty had at last been brought to book in its own lies.

Modern materialism and the personality drives fed by propaganda had created a world where everyone's personal values were oriented to themselves alone. Self-interest became the only interest. Remorse ceased to have meaning. The inevitable outcome of material prosperity without any leavening of spiritual prosperity came in the ultimate breakdown of all loyalties save those of self-interest.

This Ulcer Culture developed on its own juices, frighteningly complacent, decadent with jollity, harping on misfortune, caring only for self-indulgence, pitiful and contemptuous and yet so logical and inevitable that it transcended any normal feelings of revulsion because it became the accepted norm. When men and women, through the machinations of politicians and the demands of big business only slightly held back, saw around them a world in which their vote had become a cipher, their control on their leaders non-existent, their control even of their working conditions rapidly fading away, when ordinary people saw all this the effort of it all became not worth the rewards. Why worry? Why bother?

Inevitably, ordinary people turned to other sources of satisfaction and gratifications for the bodily drives they, as members of the human race, had been blessed and cursed with. When all around them ordinary life became what would have been to earlier generations a mockery and a blasphemy against all that mankind had struggled for, the people of the new world danced and drank and fornicated and drugged – most of all, they drugged.

Adolf Eric Sturm knew all this old history better than most. He had used his knowledge when he had battered his way up the ladder of success. He did not remember but he knew about those early days when men's consciences began to die. A man, walking a city street, seeing a pretty girl, would not hesitate to rape her for his own gratification if he could. Only the presence

80

of others who might kill him would deter him. Only the knowledge that others might be breaking into his house even as he was breaking into his neighbour's stopped him from wholesale looting. The patterns had settled down in bloody foam.

Eventually people had banded uneasily together to form insurance companies that would protect their members and exact vengeance. Scientific technology had devised ways of information. People died off and the population decreased. The years of stagnation and decay crept along.

And the Uppers tapped their Joy Juice and took their jolts and the workers dozed in the drugged stupors. And life on Earth continued.

The general trend of industrial civilisation had indeed trended well. Not one avenue of advancement had been overlooked. Nothing had been undone that should have been done. Everything had been done and everything had worked splendidly, so that civilisation in the end choked in its own excreta.

Although not a true picture, this view indicated enough truths to illustrate what had happened. Not everyone had gone entirely to the bad. Although, Sturm had often reflected, it would have been much simpler if they had. These Moral Aid people now wanted to ban the use of lucimechs. Ridiculous! Stick to the old and well-worn drugs, they proclaimed, strong in the armour of virtue. If you can get a lift from the old faithful, why try to take a trip by machine? They had caused some trouble, too. Lucimechs still had not caught on fully in some areas. People always had been conservative, preferring to coast along on the drugs they knew.

The government had long since stopped all that nonsense of drug companies fiddling about with the molecular arrangements of well-known drugs, copping a patent, and fleecing the public. Now all drugs – everything, more or less – had been controlled by the government. Not that the government cared much either way, they mostly spent their individual time taking trips; but things had a habit of happening as they always did and different people did a job every now and then and, somehow, the whole crazy fabric staggered on.

Sturm, as an ambitious man outside hallucinations, had no desire to enter government.

As the last and – hell, yes! – greatest art collector the world had ever known he rested secure in the knowledge that his niche in history was inviolable.

'As to why we're on this world at all,' said Zack Conrad grumpily to Dirk Havergen as they walked out to the battered electric car sagging in the yard. 'no one knows and anyone who tries to tell you he does know is a liar.'

'But surely – ' said Havergen with vague memories, Conrad guessed, of ancient religious theories clashing and ringing in his head like clapperless bells.

'If there ever was a God, and that's as proper a belief as any humanist belief that there wasn't, then He must have packed it in long ago under the weight of humanity's jeering disbelief.' Conrad opened the door carefully and got in, sinking well back on soft springing. Havergen drove again. Conrad became aware that the empty seat to the rear wanted to engulf him in melancholy, to drag his mind into unwanted fear-fantasies. He said belligerently: 'If you said that man killed God I reckon you'd be right.'

'If there ever was a God to be killed,' Havergen said, letting the electric motors in and steering the car out through the folded-back gates on to the street. One wing just nudged the metal gate, screeching.

'You stupid oaf,' Conrad said, turning his head. 'We don't have many cars left.'

'Sturm said – ' began Havergen.

'Don't!' Conrad's immediate reaction surprised him. He could not shake his mind free from that picture of Sturm, black-bristle-headed, pugnacious of jaw and poignarding of eye, glaring out at him from the screen with cowing force. Sturm's not happy over Vincent. And then Tony Lawrence – ' He shook his head and, with the prospect of a half-hour's journey before him, fired up the Ack-Ack gun. He lay back with a cigarette, dragging in the raw smoke, letting Havergen goose-pimple with unslaked dryness.

'You're a right bastard, Zack,' Havergen said at last.

The man amused Conrad, feeling the black tide of frustration at his handling by Sturm. Everyone was a bastard to everyone else, everyone knew that, and yet the old opprobriums remained, anachronistic, persistent.

'You drive, Dirk.' He blew smoke tantalisingly.

Havergen had the sense to keep on going. Sturm stood as a

giant shadow behind Conrad and ordinary conduct here would have brought swift interinsurance justice.

On the thought both men glanced up at the Insurance Tower. On the outskirts of the general Upper city limits and a scant hundred yards from the end of the all-embracing roof, the tower jutted gauntly for an unadorned height of seven hundred feet. Above that columned shaft the crew quarters and garages began, extending upwards another three hundred feet. Above them the badge detectors and electronics occupied a further hundred and fifty feet. Aerials with their universal semblance to interpenetrated constructivist sculptural forms flowered in a maze of metal above.

'They fell down on the job last night,' said Havergen with a viciousness not concealing his anger and fear.

Conrad shared that fear. If the Insurance Assessors failed to apprehend and exact vengeance then where lay their much vaunted security?

Someone working on an aerial arm, suspended in the morning breeze by a plastic-nylon safety belt, waved an arm down to them. His dark figure looked like a marionette, hung against the bright sky, light eroded.

'Idiot,' said Havergen, making it unnecessary for Conrad to add anything, in the normal way.

Then, seeing a chance to score in the game, he said: 'Perhaps not. He was probably making rude signs at us.'

Havergen concentrated on his driving.

Through the avenues of the old city they drove at a sedate speed, the ancient automobile splay-footed, the tyres now all repaired and plump, but dispirited.

They passed beneath the first of the mammoth overhead ways, the side supports and railings seemingly as strong and rigid as the day they had been built; but the central roadway had long since fallen through in ragged gaps leaving a double-toothpick of rot-gapped teeth stretching from one side of the avenue to the other.

The Ack-Ack gun had been firing steadily for Conrad now and he swooned off a trifle, listlessly. He could take a quick snifter like this for as long as a boring interlude supervened because his system, like anyone else's, could cope with drugs. In the old days a man would have been right gone sent and out of this world on the weed taken by Conrad. The Uppers permitted this among themselves mainly because anyone did what anyone wanted if not too many others, or the Insurance Company, objected; but they had firmly squashed the habit among the workers, ruthlessly. What – allow a worker to squander all that precious joy effluvia? What rubbish! No Upper was going to allow waste of that sort, not saga-ing likely.

Conrad sucked and blew and then Havergen said tartly: 'Coming up to the Avenue of the Spheres now. Looks quiet.'

Reluctantly, Conrad allowed himself to regain consciousness of his surroundings. They appeared hateful to him; the openness, the rounded-fronts of the buildings leering at him as though daring him to unimaginable follies.

The car halted clumsily at the intersection where last night – where, last night, Tony Lawrence had alighted looking for fun and had found, instead, his last trip of all.

'This where – ' began Havergen.

'We'd better go back further,' Conrad cut across, the memory of Sturm's eyes on him uncomfortably pressing. 'We finished up at a joint called Aladdin or something. We'd better take over from there.'

'Does it matter?' Havergen started the car again.

Past the ziggurats of herculean architecture the car crawled like a black beetle; mass of steel and concrete and glass raking into the morning sky, level after level of smooth pavement blank and empty, echoing to no cry, swept bleak and bare, decaying and abandoned. The city stunted the spirit. The city cried aloud with an eloquent silent plea. Here all the dreams of futurists of long ago had come to fruition and held their sway and dropped away and been forgotten.

'Sturm says if we don't find Vincent we're going to be in trouble.' Conrad glanced uneasily up at the blue and ochre and chrome buildings, so tall, frowning with the look of a moronic child down upon the canyons between their lifeless bodies. 'We could all end up like this.'

'So let's find Vincent,' said Havergen, slamming the door. The car winced. They left it there today; no worker would take it because no worker would have a use for an automobile, and today they did not have Tony Lawrence with them.

Passing beneath the monolithic and crumbling façade of the Technocracy Building, its many levels nude of helicopters and fliers, its myriad windows like eyes put out, blank, its columned shafts pitted with years, they walked, two small men, towards the shadows of the farther wall. Here a sign winked gaily at them, bright and insouciant and modern.

LILY'S LULLABY
THE SWITCHED ON LUCIMECH LAIR

Conrad noticed with malicious amusement how Havergen's face flushed up and his hands clenched.

'Feeling troubled, Dirk?' he asked with spiteful concern. This one was a giggle. Even Lawrence hadn't known this. Poor old Tony, the fool, dead and gone and never again able to take a trip or to sip Joy Juice.

'Troubled?' snapped Havergen, nettled. 'Of course I'm not. I just don't like the atmosphere of these kind of places.'

He would have gone on, but Conrad, jauntily, walked off, heading towards the garish sign.

Some attempts had been made at luring trade here. Any worker could go to any tripjoint or lucimech palace and almost invariably he would head for the nearest. But strange fads and fancies had grown up – they existed even among the Uppers – and a man would passionately believe that one type of drug, one couch, a special pattern of lucimech, some intricate way of composing himself for the experience, would give him the boom of heightened impressions, greater freedoms, more reality on his trips.

Lily, whoever she might be and if she even existed any more, had catered for this taste in her clients. There were small individual touches about the place to brighten it and bring more attention to bear on this reality as well as the reality of the trip. A couple of workers with their heads bowed and shoulders bent walked swiftly into the place as the two Uppers approached, sparing them no glance, intent on one thing only in this world.

'Lucimechs!' said Havergen, the word a small curse.

'Well, naturally!' Conrad said, feeling fine, feeling that the game had swung his way and that he need spare no pity for Havergen. 'Hallucinofabs may well replace drugs entirely, one day.'

Havergen swung on him, his face congested, eyes like buttons. 'You debased saga'd degenerate! Anyone knows that drugs are the only natural way, the only clean way, to take a trip!

Why, if I had my way all this would be ripped down, burnt, destroyed, wiped out – ' He was panting and a fleck of foam flicked from his lips.

Conrad chuckled.

This was first rate. He'd really got this fool going.

'You ought to try a lucimech hallucination, one day, Dick,' he said gently, with the full effect of wooden-spooning, and loving it.

Havergen spat at him. Literally. He missed. Conrad's hand dropped to his gun butt; then he laughed sourly. Havergen, too, had half drawn.

'Your chances of staying alive, Havergen, aren't so good today as they were yesterday. Remember, the man who killed Tony Lawrence is still at large!'

'And that goes for you too!' Havergen had finally sloughed off his feeling of inferiority. Conrad knew why. Sturm had given him a job to do of equal status to Conrad's. But that wouldn't stop a bullet in the back. The fool had been too presumptuous and now – now the dolt had spat at him. Conrad shoved his gun back and left it loose and ready for instant action. Words were part of the game; but when the game broke down then the old arguments regained their ancient force.

Together, shoulder to shoulder but not touching, the two men walked up the steps and under the sign proclaiming Lily's attractions to dopey-eyed workers. The shadow bit beneath the arch. Their footsteps rang with loud authority on the concrete.

No one sat in the reception booth where the pale luminescence of control panels told of a computer in use that should have been broken-up and distributed years ago.

'These damn places,' fumed Havergen. 'That cyber probably misses more cogs than a punch-card dog-eared index.'

'Yes,' said Conrad, in his needling sceptical voice. 'These palaces aren't like tripjoints – but I suppose you'd know all about that.' He fleered his eyes at Havergen, walking with an erectness about his collar and neck that gave Conrad some small joy. The man was like a kettle on the boil, all ready to steam into explosion.

'They should never be allowed to join the Ring,' Havergen said with righteous viciousness. 'Then they'd soon find out who's right.'

'How a man like you can believe all the guff the Moral Aid nitwits churn out is beyond me,' said Conrad with some real feeling. He had seen the Moral Aid manifestos, and laughed along with everyone else – or, nearly everyone else, for, quite evidently, Dirk Havergen had been got at by Moral Aid.

Havergen did not reply. Conrad kept his hand on his gun, just in case he had.

They stopped by the computer. The cybernetic circuits showed in full operation, green lights outnumbered red, amber or dead lights. There was not too much dust dulling the surfaces. Someone, apparently, looked in every now and then. They walked on.

The first hallucinofab they reached was unoccupied; but at the second machine with its orbiting ring of couches, the two workers they had seen enter were about to succumb. They lowered their bodies with rapid stiff precision, like puppets whose strings were being clumsily disentangled, both their faces avid and suffused with thirst. Everyone alive knew that feeling, that look, that desperate sensation of intolerable dryness. The world had failed these men, as it had failed Conrad and Havergen, and all the world could offer now was a couch and a dream.

In the vast effusion of time the fixed flux of those dreaming moments held some remnant of reason, some dimly-perceived answer to a question no man dared ask.

Conrad and Havergen passed down the outer circle of couches, unobserved, observing, seeking in each gaunt and abstracted face for the features of Vincent, the beard, the rough thickness of lip and chin. They very carefully did not look at the hallucinofab. Not to look, in Conrad's case, posed a diabolical temptation, for he felt the need to slough off this stupid world-reality and find the true inner mind-reality of his own hallucinations. But Sturm, for sure, would have this place bugged.

For Havergen, the lucimechs posed only the problem of avoidence, of contamination, of abhorrence. For Havergen the putrid moral codes and outworn shibboleths of Moral Aid had bitten deeply and turned his desires into a self-torture, so that what was natural became pitifully distorted for him into what was sinful. Hell! Conrad didn't like Havergen and had made up his mind to kill the fool as soon as a suitable opportunity arose – no one was going to spit at him with impunity – but Havergen merely represented a whole group of limited intellects who allowed moral perverts to tell them that only drugs were natural and hallucinofabs were immoral, obscene and sinful.

In the centre of the ring of couches the lucimech ran through its paces, coloured lights aswirl, bowls of luminescence, whirling dots of alternate colour and vibration, drawing a man's mind out thin, like taffy fresh from the boil.

'How refreshing, to dive brain-first into that!' Conrad meant it.

'You dissipated degenerate!' Havergen savaged a man's head out from under his shielding arm, thrust it pettishly back. 'Where the saga-ing hell is Vincent?'

The machine, having finished with the two newcomers on their couches, having sent them into shadowed caverns and brilliant uplands, giving them the opportunity to explore the landscapes of their minds, clicked shortly to itself with satisfaction, switched itself off. The lights dimmed.

No one had as yet found a satisfactory formula for the universal passage through this consciousness that every man and woman must make; but the hallucinomechs offered a substitute. The inner landscapes of the mind lit and bedecked by drugs so that the psyche could inturn and enter and delight offered a slick and understandable formula. With me, said every hallucination, you are safe.

Thinking wistfully of his last trip, of the purple inverted mountains, their peaks lodestones of snowy desires, Conrad thumbed through the workers on their couches. Sturm, he guessed, had his place adequately bugged, the broadcast signals streaming into his room like lemmings on a cinema-film re-run backwards. Sturm had his fingers on the pulse – trouble was, the patient was dying.

'Vincent's not here,' he said disgustedly, reaching the last lucimech, an older and more cumbrous model, suitable for teenagers. Four girls sprawled out around it, and two boys, all wearing grey and brown patterned smocks, all stained and greasy. Little sexual differences appeared between the girls and boys; hair short, smocks, spindly legs. Small pointed tufts of cloth alone promised Conrad's impromptu sexing as accurate observation. For young chits of girls like this Conrad had as much sexual feeling as he might have for the grey-haired old crone guarding that terrible tripjoint he had visited yesterday. Little girls were for little boys, whenever the Uppers decided the time was right. Although, he had heard – rumours – that Sturm liked a little little. Sturm. Hell, yes, if they didn't find Arthur Vincent Cheesman soon, Sturm had said, they'd all be in trouble of such seriousness they'd never recover. Ever.

'Any luck?' he shouted angrily at Havergen. The fat man was bending down beneath a machine. He was, Conrad saw with shock, actually touching the metal of what was to him a blasphemous artifact of sin.

'Moral Aid will be after you, Friend!'

Havergen glanced up. His face showed dark and congested.

'Look at this, will you, you prettified – '

'Don't say it, Havergen!'

'Come and look at this, for all sagas' sake!'

Clumsily, Conrad walked across. He looked down. He drew in his breath sharply making a thin whistle in the lucimech lair. 'Sturm must be told at once!'

The two men changed, their features hardened and planed out into lines of ruthlesness. Their movements became quick and assured. Conrad pulled out his belt radio and called Sturm's room, being put through at once. Speaking with his lips close to the microphone, he said: 'Sturm! This is Zack Conrad. We are in Lily's Lullaby – near the bottom end of the Avenue of Spheres. The Joy effluvia connections have been broken – '

'Stay right where you are!' Sturm's brittle words clicked glottally from the speaker. 'A Revenue team will get down to you right away.'

Another of the few precious fliers left would be leaping from Revenue Tower, the rearing twin colossus to Insurance Tower, up there at the end of the spanning comforting roof over Upper town. It would be cleaving the bright morning air towards them, careening cleanly through the wider channels between the recessed ziggurat levels of the old city. Angry men, grim-faced men, cheated men, would be aboard. Any minute now –

'Let's go outside and meet them,' said Conrad jerkily.

8

Diogenes rapped on his barrel to call Smith's attention.

'You would like some more sausage?'

'No thank you.' The man whose name was Diogenes but who liked to be called Gray silently indicated a pile of toothpicks on the counter. Smith handed a packet across. Gray went to work with needling thoroughness.

'Not many dentists like to take time out to visit me in my barrel,' he said, without rancour.

'What's the situation – outside?' Smith made of the question a tentative proposal.

'Oh, I can tell you all about that sort of thing,' Good humour beamed as the toothpick notched in and out in time to the words spoken. I keep in touch.'

'Yes.'

'It the Pill, you know.'

'Oh?'

'Making people re-think their obligations and priorities.'

'Priorities?'

'Favourite word. Fave word, I suppose I should say. Get your priorities right. That means having a statutory two and a half children per family and not asking for a wage increase before the other fellow.'

'But – the Pill – ?' Smith was enjoying this.

'Guilt, old man. Absolutely spiffing guilt, you know. Why, the Bomb had nothing on this. The Bomb was dropped by some poor guys thinking they were helping to win the War. Thousands of miles away. Best you could do was get into a march about it. But the Pill – ! Oh, ho!'

'Oh, ho?'

'You tell the missis to use it, she says, "I wanna babee!" You suggest you would like a child, the girl friend says: 'You slob – I'm taking the Pill." Gives you a personal sense of power, does the Pill. Up to you if you want a new life or not. Better than a hundred thousand incinerated and irradiated corpses any day.'

'You were talking about horror – '

'Horror conventions, atrocity exhibitions, strip shows, they're all in it together. Why do you think the poor slobs of the mid-twentieth century got so hot under the collar about atrocity – bomb victims, torture victims in Africa, concentration camp victims, napalm victims in Vietnam? Why? I'll tell you. They wanted victims. They hadn't seen any horror, any atrocities for too long. The sight of a radiation victim should have made them squeal – it did – the sight of twiggy arms and legs in Buchenwald made them squeal – they should. How many cared to dwell on the pictures that came out of the Great War, out of Spain, out of China before the second coming of the Beast? So few they could not prepare these kids around for real horror.'

'You do go on,' said Smith politely.

'And with reason. Atrocity exhibitions became fashionable because people had forgotten what life is really like, what it is about. Ehrlich's silver bullet or magic bullet cleaned up a lot of venereal disease. Very few mid-twentieth-century men and women had seen the atrocity of a woman's face suffering from pustular syphiloderma.'

'I have seen wax models – ' Smith said with dignity.

'Sure. But not many ordinary men and women knew what disease was really like – medicine had accomplished much. Concentration camps and radiation and napalm damage came through mass media as bolts from a sunny sky. No wonder atrocities became a vogue.'

'And they added another kick to a decaying society.'

'Precisely. Because people claimed more freedom from the old disciplines – and rightly too, I suppose, it could be argued – they saw more clearly. And the more clearly they saw the more they understood how little they were, of what microscopic importance in the scheme of things. Of no importance at all, if you ask me.'

'I am, as you will observe, asking you,' Smith said, hiding his delighted chuckle.

'People began to wake up to the unpalatable fact that they were mere organisms squiggling on the object glass of the world – and who was studying them? No one – since they had rejected all ideas of God.'

'All ideas?'

'Well, any ideas designed to give them comfort. They stripped off their swaddling clothes of innocent belief and faced the hostile universe naked. And they just could not accept the truth – if they had indeed found that elusive lady. That the meaning of all life was meaningless became a very popular theme in the mid-century – but it destroyed what men had striven for for centuries and it destroyed the image of man in men.'

'I can see it would.'

'Oh, it did. A mere cog in the machinery wasn't going to take much interest in the machinery unless he was well rewarded. Unfortunately, the classes remained apart and the rewards did not accrue.'

Smith could have gone on talking for some time on these lines. He was well aware – none better, in fact – that these ideas had been implanted in his mind in quick snatches when he was young. Everyone these days – these days back in his own reality where he lay on one of Guztav Lawlor's couches – received pre-hallucinatory teaching. Films were fired off at children, reel after glamorous reel, spinning through the eyes and into the mind so fast, like buckshot of culture straight from creator to grey cells, palpitating with tumescence. The children didn't learn anything at once from these dream-fodder experiences. Down and down into the mind they settled, quiescent, waiting, artful. Then – then on any trip that child subsequently took among the grottoes of its own brain, these old facts, fancies, concepts, arguments, landscapes, would spring forth in full sparkle, spangle, glittershow immediacy.

Like Diogenes, now, re-telling the miasma of self-interest and self-blindness that destroyed that old mid-twentieth century civilisation and paved the way for the age of Material Plenty. That had blown itself up, too, although Smith was not as certain how that had happened.

He drank the rest of his Tizer and refilled the glass, and

opened his mouth, ready to contest with the man in the tub the position of the artist in a world from which the shades had fallen.

He remained with his mouth open. Then, hurriedly, he snapped his teeth together.

Advancing towards him between ranks of laughing teenagers, happy in their bare chests and miniskirts – boys as well as girls – stalked the sinuous yellow and black leopard-woman. She carried her tail mincingly. Her half mask set a jet surround to the wasp-flames of her eyes. Her midnight blue gown sequined and spangled as she moved in a ripplingly effortless glide. Among all these near-sexless boys and girls she glowed and coruscated like an enormous evil jewel.

Smith set down his drink, slopping, clutched the rim of Diogenes' tub.

'I say old fruit, everything all right?'

'I thought I was safely in an hallucination. I can't be down a further stage, surely? But I must be – '

'Must be what, old chum? Another sausage?'

'I must be in an hullucination within an hallucination. Where this happened – what began it – how – I cannot tell – '

The catwoman smiled blasphemously as she advanced. Her scarlet lips opened a ripe seduction, an invitation to bliss that scorched.

Smith debated, very carefully, very sagaciously – and very damn quickly.

After Smith there could be Jones, or Brown, or Robinson – omitting the Crusoe of that ilk – or any of the many still-persisting other-language variations, LeBlanc, Muller, Moskowitz. All solid and safe and reliable. But – but he was a man who created, who moulded hallucinations. He controlled the input. He mixed the drugs, he set the hallucinofab mechanisms winking.

His own pride, dead though such outmoded words were these days, his own awkwardness, his own bloody-mindedness, of which there was much these days, demanded that he stay here and find out what was going wrong. He stiffened himself up and glared at the leopard-woman and mentally told her to get the hell out of it. Unruffled, undisturbed, she glided on.

'Go away!' he said harshly.

Her lips leered with scarlet passion at him. The tips of her teeth showed, white and hard and sharp, like fangs.

He pulled a little back, set Diogenes' tub between him and the blue sequined dress. She glided around it with a swing of hips. Her jewelled gloved hands reached out to him.

'Go away! Get off!'

She touched him. One finger resting with white fire against his cheek, coy, the brand-mark of the devil, did his business for him.

He ran.

Fleet pattering footsteps followed him. Weaving in and out of the dancers in that high hall, the leopard-woman followed him with feminine remorselessness, following, following. . . .

This was his hallucination, wasn't it? He groped in his pocket for a gun. His hands encountered crumbs and dust and a spent bus ticket, The Pantiles to Pembury. How could this be his own hallucination? Hadn't he entered this world through a strange subterranean half-seen half-sensed other world of sea-green dimness? He had had no control of himself. He had none now. In his own mind he ran and ran and sweat started out on his forehead at the slithering menace of the catwoman relentlessly following him.

Well, then, Jones?

Jones.

JONES!

The revenue men swore vilely as they raced into Lily's Lullaby. They hit the pavement before the flier stopped and they swarmed into the lucimech palace with guns in their fists and tight ugly expressions of hatred on their faces. There were a dozen of them. Their boots made a great noise.

Havergen, eager, showed them.

The Revenue men clustered around the severed connections. They wore black tight uniforms – uniform in the true sense of the word in that their outfits were the same one with the other – and globular quasi-jet pilots' helmets, with the scarlet letter 'R' emblazoned on the front and both sides. R for Revenue. At the back of each helmet the words, smaller, had been stencilled: 'Department of Inland Revenue.'

Their leader, an orange-faced man with a concave chest that did no justice to the tight black tunic, kicked the nearest worker. The worker moved and then groaned and then flopped back as he had been before.

'Get them all out of here,' he snapped tartly to his men. At once the revenuers began hoisting the hallucinated workers up, dragging them out by the heels, their back hairs scraping the concrete, uncaring. 'Where's Lily?'

'Is there such a female?' asked Conrad. 'There is a computer.'

The orange-faced leader back-handed Conrad across the mouth.

'Speak when you're spoken to, punk. And keep a civil tongue in your head.'

Conrad glared with eyes that disembowelled, shredded, flayed, debrained, de – Conrad stared with quivering lips and shaking jaw and eyes that showed red.

And, in that instant of hatred . . .

. . . the leader and he, fast locked in slime, alone and yet always with the other chained to the other, mud and filth creeping up their legs, their waists, their chests, slopping at their chins and mouths . . .

Conrad slumped back, shaking.

The leader jerked as though touched by a high tension cable. His pig-like eyes went mean. He shook speech out of himself like a dog scratching out fleas.

'You swine! Get outta here! Get out fast! If you give me another damn newdism I'll kill you! *Get out!*'

There was nothing in this situation Conrad could do or say save get out. Shaking, hardly able to control his muscles, his face like blotting paper, he went out.

Havergen laughed at him.

A loose slobbering wheezing sound blubbered from Conrad. 'The Insurance Company is going to have an unlucky streak before long,' he kept saying to himself, over and over, as he trickled limply down the steps and out on to the paving stones of the forecourt. 'Unlucky streak – streak – reak – that was it – wreak! Wreak vengeance – for no one spoke to another in that fashion these days without rue. Rue and wreak and blood . . . ' His thoughts spiralled helplessly. He walked on, not seeing where he was going, his mind inwardly directed to his planned vengeance.

Some stupefied worker had thrown a knife at Tony

Lawrence and killed him and not been aprehended and vengeance taken. Well, then. Surely he, Zack Conrad, could do more than a simple single-named worker? Surely?

Sturm?

Sturm had reached his eminence as Insurer of his Company by ruthless concentration. It had brought great and rewarding dividends. Of the other Insurance Companies in the city few, if any, could match the Sturm Insurance Company for size and power. These Revenuers, now, from the government-maintained Revenue Tower – they belonged to half a dozen Insurance Companies, as their badges testified. Well then. Conrad's face showed clearly the trend of his thoughts; his hand squeaked on the walnut of his gunbutt just as had Lawrence's.

Sturm had called in the Inland Revenue; Sturm wouldn't care, wouldn't even think about it, if one of his Company killed a Revenuer; his only concern would be for the decedent's Insurance Company, if they could catch their man, make a kill-for-kill policy settlement.

Conrad halted in the shadow of a stained concrete pillar, the ferrous rusting showing through like the stains of dried blood, looked back at Lily's Lullaby.

The Revenuers' flier, its vanes and ground-effect hoods silent and motionless, waited by the kerb. Havergen stood just outside the first doors, and Conrad saw with a quick stab of envy, the man was creasing his sliver of silver paper, readying himself to take the Dream of the Golden Dragon as soon as he could find a quiet spot. Havergen had nerve, goofing off like that when Sturm had given the orders. But Conrad – anyone – knew how he felt.

These old-time drug habits died hard; marijuana, for instance, was like eating a bar of candy to the men of Conrad's day; but that did not mean they did not enjoy hemp, or mescalin or the old disappointment, lysergic acid. They kept them going, a sort of snack between meals, until they could hit their couch and take a real trip. Conrad watched Havergen move into the shadows and then walked calmly but with quivering nerves towards the abandoned pile of workers.

He bent as he reached the sprawl of arms and legs, and with a quick and thrillingly nervous movement searched for and found three workers' knives. These, with a swift movement, he secreted beneath his shirt. Then he walked on, his feet uncomfortably loud on the paving flags, his back erect and his brow sweaty.

He waited in the shadows beyond the first archway, looking back into the sunshine where the workers' bodies contorted a motion-sculpture from frozen immobility.

The memory of why he was here, the importance of finding Vincent, occurred to him, to be summarily flung back into the limbo of forgotten trivia. He knew why he was *here*.

Lean black forms moved at the door and then a clump of Revenue men with among them a sagging smock-covered worker, heels dragging, striated with energetic gestures the sunlight of the entrance. Conrad watched hungrily. The Revenuers hauled their prisoner along like a sack. She yammered shrilly, protesting; but even Conrad could hear the vacuous undertone of appalled defeat.

'You'll answer to the Ring, Lily, and they'll crucify you.'

'You get a licence and what do you do – you switch off the joy effluvia – '

'You'll be stretched for this, Lily.'

The Revenue Officers, evidently, were enjoying themselves. No doubt most of them had had to be dragged away from a trip or the beginning of a trip, and now they were going to kick the most likely target. One target already kicked lowered in the shadows and gripped a hating fist on the haft of a worker's knife.

Conrad began to notice the environment about him that he understood to be reality with almost the same crystal clarity and detail as he saw objects in an hallucination.

The precise and particular colouration of the striations in the stone flags; the way the concrete stained a mouldy brown as it decayed; the patterns the sunlight threw from twisted rusting girders; the way the air smelled, clean and absinthe-clear, unpolluted. He noticed things he had not bothered to notice this way before.

Most of all he saw the way the orange-faced leader swaggered a little apart from his men, ordering, gesturing, contemptuous lips mobile in the hatred that was his face.

Carefully, Conrad wiped his fingerprints from the knives; carefully he slid his right hand into the glove he took from its pocket on his belt, alongside the radio. With the exquisite sensation reserved for other moments of fundamental truths he lifted the blade. The metal, through the gossamer-thin gloves, felt hard and ridged and right.

He thought, fleetingly, of Lawrence and of the worker who had thrown in that instant of challenge.

Well, this orange-faced baboon would not receive that amount of warning. . . .

He threw.

He felt the biting hunger of wanting to wait and see the knife strike. He felt the painful sensations of hunger and greed for that sight to satiate his arid senses; but he could not stay. He turned and ran. Lightly, silently, he ran all crabwise across the flags beneath the shadow of the architrave rearing ten stories above him. Out from the sunlight lean and yellow rays pierced through the slots of crumbling masonry; but he hurdled them like a swimmer, diving between coral outcrops and the spearing shafts of the ocean sun.

Around the back alley he fled, not caring for fear now, not caring to meet a worker, his gun already it seemed of its own volition in his gloved fist, not caring if Sturm himself showed with archangel magnificence. He could feel the thick and heavy gushing of his blood. He could hear the tempest echo in his ears. He felt the tremor of extreme exhaustion sublime – hel! He'd done it. He'd put that orange-faced punk down under the daisies – if anyone ever knew now what a daisy was – and he was not going to be caught. He'd done the fellow's business. Now let his Insurance Company squawk.

He cut through the back alleys and so came out on to the shadowed area where Havergen sat contemplating his own Dream of the Golden Dragon.

For the first time in his life, Zack Conrad felt the touch of reality in something he had done in this his life pierce home to him with the same impact as a hallucination. It made him think – or would have, had there been time.

'Hey, Dirk,' he said with friendly face. 'Hey, come on, Bung. We're supposed to be looking for Vincent. There's a sign down there a ways. Come on hup, Friend.'

He wondered, fleetingly, with a clinical detachment, if he had overdone it. The 'Bung' had sounded oddly out of character to this man even as he spoke.

But Havergen turned a dulled cod-fish eye up, smoke drifting reeking around his nostrils.

'Sure,' he said, slowly. 'Sure. Just let me finish this Dragon off – Friend.'

So.

So now maybe he would not be suspected when he stuck the knife in this fool's back.

He could despatch him right now, of course.

But Conrad felt with justice that he had not abandoned all claim on rationality when he took vengeance. The Revenue man dead, and Havergen dead, and Conrad not accounted for – that would make a tough swallow. Better this way, this clever way, with the Revenue bastard dead and Havergen as a witness that Conrad had been here out of harm's way. Oh yes, much better. . . .

Later, Havergen.

Later, for you, the knife, you fool.

Coughing and sneezing enough to show he had been away for a spell, Havergen followed Conrad out of that secluded pool of shadow beside the shattered wall into the sunlight of the Avenue of Spheres. The Revenuers were clustered around their leader like dry workers around a hallucinofab that had gone on the blink. Conrad glanced at the crowded black backs.

'Hullo,' he said. 'Something up?' He was loving this. He was enjoying this, every splendid moment of it. He thought of that orange-faced fool and the loathsome newdism and he pressed on anxious to see just where the knife had penetrated. He wished, he admitted frankly, he wished to see blood and smell the satisfying smokiness of it.

'They're in a two and eight,' said Havergen blearily.

'What's up, then?' asked Conrad of the nearest black back.

He never learned, it seemed.

The black back swung around to reveal the congested baboon-face of a Revenue officer, passionate and vengeful. A hand lashed out, struck Conrad around the mouth, pitched him sprawling back on to the concrete.

'Get to hell outta this, creep! This is Reven*oo* biz!'

Again, Havergen laughed.

From the sunshine hot pavement, Conrad glared up with the spittle and the blood drooling down his chin, his breath panting and hoarse, gasping with the terrible effort of doing nothing.

'The main problem today is one of communication,' said the neat, dark man in the white coat, a stethoscope around his neck and the latest copy of 'New Poetry' sticking out of one pocket. 'Communication theory and getting to understand what the other fellow is up to – that's what it's all about today, that's what makes the scene this whirl of the time stream.'

'Old rope,' said the man who had, for reasons best left unsaid, decided to call himself Jones. 'Who cares about communication? *I* don't want to get to know my neighbour. Communication? Are you crazy?'

'The problem of social attitudes, the problems of pain and communication, I repeat, are the in thing – '

'They may be in with you, mac, but they're way out and ready to drop out for me.' Jones chuckled, there in the blue and purple shot darkness, the white, rose-red tinted wall comfortably at his elbow, the glass of wine on the scrubbed board table before him. 'If you'd ever experienced a nudism you'd know that communication is not what the masses want.'

The man in the white coat sipped his own ruby wine, breaking a light fluffy bread roll with his other hand, his fingers long and slender and firm, a gold ring winking. Somewhere strings and woodwind drifted in a gauze of soporific music, long vowel sounds of digestion.

'If you can't get to the other fellow,' said the man in the white coat, popping a fingering of bread into his mouth, 'Hoss ger good o' ith?'

'I beg your pardon?'

'I said,' the man said, swallowing roundly: 'What's the good of it?'

'What's the good of what?'

'Tut-tut!' The man unslung his stethoscope and leaned forward. He plonked the end against Jones's white shirt front. 'Ta-ra-ra-rrrump-pump-he-pump!' said the man. 'Such beautiful music, inside the chest.'

'I usually charge a small admission fee to my heart concerts,' said Jones, happily.

'Take a piece of bread. I have the wine, and now – '

'Thou? Thee? Us?'

'Communication, you see, all at sea.'

'That's just a modern fad. If you set up a decent multi-lingual directory and dictionary and encyclopedia and have a permanent Language Culture authority, you'll soon organise understanding.' Jones tried the bread. After the sausage and Tizer with Diogenes he still felt hungry. The bread was good. Where was Diogenes now, alas? 'There is altogether too much cretinous wilful non-understanding in the world,' he finished with a self-righteousness that afforded him a comforting giggle. This was better.

'You say that, you who organised Joy Juice?'

'I didn't organise it. That happened a long time ago.' Jones sighed in maudlin sorrow, drank more wine. 'But had I had that opportunity – ah! – what a glorious heroic task that would have been.' He drank with a flourish.

'The workers don't know?'

'I don't give a damn if they know or not. If they want their dope or their hallucinomechs, then they donate their juice effluvia – or else.'

'But suppose somebody, right now, someone in Guztav Lawlor's place, was draining *you*?'

'What?' Jones overset his wine glass. Like blood the spilled wine spread across the scrubbed boards. 'Me! No one would dare!'

'You see – you are alarmed and outraged. Perhaps Sturm –'

'I'll see him saga'd first! No – that would be too good for the bum! I'll –' Jones stood up unsteadily, feeling the floor heaving beneath his feet. The orchestra played syrupy soft. The man in the white coat smiled up, assured, aloof, the embodiment of all men in white coats.

'I know your sort!' Jones said, swaying giddily. 'Men in white coats with cheque-books for hearts! Doctors who have sold their souls to drug companies! I know you – drug promoters who develop some piddling little variation in someone else's drug, and then advertise it, and sell it, and devil take the consequences! You don't give a damn about causing fatal iatrogenic illness so long as your shareholders wax fat. You tell filthy lies about your wares, and then go on telling them until at last decent people tell you to shut up, after they've seen the side-effects, the lesions, the limbless, the jaundiced, the dead.'

'My, my,' said the man in the white coat with a reverberating mocking echo, 'you do go on.'

'It's about time, here in your civilisation, for a stand to be taken, for the drug companies to have their wings clipped, their money rationalised – research does not absorb the money you claim it does – your whole existence is that of the vampire – battening on human misery!'

'You sound indignant, you, who drain like a super-vampire the life spirits from the working classes – '

'That's different! We don't cheat the workers, we don't claim to cure them and kill them instead – '

'But, my dear – Smith, was it? – doctors have been doing that since the first man fell out of a tree!'

'I'm not talking about doctors! They do what they can – I'm talking about money-grubbing drug promoters who should be put against a wall – '

'Like me, ducky?' The voice swung Smith's head around.

The girl smiled at him with wide sickliness, a pale greasy-luminous lipstick giving her mouth the look of a lanced boil. Her hair towered in a grotesque beehive of blonde nylon hairpieces. Her face, white and slavic, looked like a roly-poly pudding set with currants within vast black hoops for eyes, with that sickly mouth mawking at him. She wore a glittery bodice, demurely cut, and fish-net tights that ended above her hipbones. Her garters had not been polished that morning. She held a tray around her middle, supported by straps from her neck, with a tiny light shining on its contents.

'I've got them all here,' she said to Smith. 'What would you care for?'

At first he thought she was that early-twentieth century phenomenon, the so-called cigarette girl, invented, he had heard, by a firm called Ouida; but on closer inspection he saw the nature of her wares. She sold cigarettes, all right, the cigarettes of adulterated drugs, of various kinds, and each bearing its slang-name of the moment, a name that changed with the age-groups of the users and pushers, that changed at the whims of taste and fear. Silver glittered in a demure pile, ready for the Dream of the Golden Dragon. Friction matchboxes, their trays all pushed out, stood nearby, ready to assist in playing the mouth organ. She carried no hypodermic needles, that Smith could see; but with a stab of nostalgia he saw the bundle of drinking straws, the blobs of drug at their ends, and remembered happy days of youth, before his parents thought him old enough to take the mainline. The girl even had a few samples of LSD, badly packed.

'You're not still on that old rubbish?' he said, involuntarily. LSD, in his own time, was merely a swear-word. 'There's no profit in playing with a drug that could kill you the first time you take it, is there? Well, is there?'

'I sell the stuff, mister. I've only had four guys drop dead since I started here. That's not a bad average.'

Smith chuckled. 'Semantically hopeless; but I take your point. I don't think, just at the moment, I will indulge.' She waggled her hips at him, pushing a fast sell. 'You see,' he said, laughing. 'I'm already down in one hallucic – and I'm possibly down in two.'

'You're a funny feller and no mistake!' She moved on, not pleased. The man in the white coat laughed. 'Your high moral tone amuses me, Smith. You drain off the workers' vitality and yet you quibble over a few lives lost by taking LSD. Contradictory, what?'

'Not at all. You just haven't grown up around here, is all.'

'Hadn't you thought that the silly youngsters who take LSD don't care if they do drop dead?' Looking at the world around them – what have they to lose?'

'If they did look at the world around them, they'd see what they had to lose. Why do you think, man in a white coat, that I – I – choose my hallucinations to take place in this time, in the time before the Age of Material Plenty, in that filthy, decadent, morally rotten, wonderful and excitingly alive twentieth century? Hey?'

'It takes all kinds, dearie.'

Smith stood up, oversetting the table. He felt a febrile thrill nerving him. That wasn't funny. This was getting to him. In a way, it was like being in a torture chair, with yourself as the torturer. He had no need – no real neeed – to go on. Everything he did rebounded, everything he said was turned against him. He was being made to feel small.

The man in the white coat bent a sharp eye on him, catching his lower lip between finger and thumb. 'Look – you'd better contact Hallucinatics Anonymous. They're accustomed to dealing with people like you. They'll help. They've been doing a lot of good, lately, getting people off the habit. The hook's sharp; but they blunt it.'

'What are you talking about? Hallucinatics Anonymous?'

'When the narcotics habit takes a real hold, you're in dead lumber. You want to nip it off soonest. Here's HA's card – '

'HA?'

'Hallucinatics Anonymous. Fine people. Some have taken the turkey, some the cold goose, others the water cure. Some got off by tapering, some by complete hematologic compatibility. We've even started our own drug cycle to negate the effects of – what are you on?' He finished the question with a snap; his authority was beginning to show.

Smith laughed. 'Your twentieth century pharmaceutical industry has no conception of the drugs I use. All your therapeutics and pharmacology would be helpless even to grasp the rudiments of the drugs I use. Leave it for now. I'm late for an appointment with a lady called Daphnis.'

'Lady?'

'Not you, too. So all right then. But if you'd seen her – a great Comfort, I assure you.'

For some time now Smith had been awaiting the appearance of the leopard woman. That she would materialise in this further hallucination he had no doubts.

'I believe you are mentally sick,' said the man in the white coat. He reached around for Smith's elbow. 'You'd better come along with me.'

Smith jerked free.

Menace breathed in the purple and red-lit dimness.

He must be careful. Incarceration, a treament of clumsy antediluvian science, operations, trepanning, prefrontals, anything of this nature in this his hallucination could kill him in actuality, could drive him insane. . . .

The man in the white coat felt again for Smith's elbow. The fumbling touch sickened him. He drew back. At once the man in the white coat grew taller; before Smith's very eyes he increased his height by six inches, as though a phantom measuring rod rose behind his head, rising as his dark hair rose. With the deliberate movement of a man about to take snuff, the man in the white coat drew from his pocket the dog-eared copy of 'New Poetry'. He opened the pages at random. He glanced darning-needle like at Smith.

'I shall now read a few stanzas. You will refrain from coughing.'

Smith edged away. To run, now, would be fatal.

On the white-coated man's face muscles writhed, a pulse like a moth fluttered his skin; he suffered as he read those great lines, his fingers twitched, the fiercer light of art's neurosis played across his brow. 'Thomas,' he said with a sigh at the end. 'Very fine.'

Smith moved gently towards the door where a sign suggested he might find refuge. 'Oh yes,' he said in willing agreement. 'Very fine. But pleasant peasantry – '

The door opened as he looked and anguish struck him as three men walked sedately out, stood watching him, their hands closely clasped before them. Each man wore a white coat. Not the white coat of the white-coated man, perhaps, not so smartly-tailored, not so authoritative. But their thick and clumsy boots, the ends of serge trouser legs, indicated more surely still their function.

Smith stopped. The man in the white coat turned pages. 'If the fools will cut down aspens,' he said, severely, 'they must expect all they get. If they hadn't – '

'If they hadn't cut down the trees,' Smith said, desperately, 'we would have been the poorer. More aspens can be grown; a handful, it seems, of Binsey Poplars only. But no havoc, no poem – no destruction, no creation. He lost his aspens dear, we gained poetry for all time.'

The men closed in. Slowly, boxing the compass, they ringed him in, closer and closer.

Gently, with a practised art, the man in the white coat took out a hypodermic needle. His three assistants, in their turn, took out their apparatus of authority, of restraint.

9

'. . . and the water was spent in the bottle.'

What words in the world of physical feeling could be worse than those?

What other words in the world of physiology could so minutely terrorise in a xerographic landscape of horror?

Sheldon knew. Sheldon crawled through mica sands with the flesh stripped from his knees and palms, his hair hanging down lank and coarse before his face, his neck stretching with fatigue, his eyes fried in their sockets.

He must go on and on, for even the double-island and its blasphemous molochian mouth would be better than this.

He could not now any longer evade the central issue. This was a hallucination, wherein he had expected – well, the usual dream aspirations that were more real than outer reality. He had been confidently anticipating good food, rich wines, beautiful and willing women, the whole gamut of the reality of his inward mind that made of the world of the factory and the canteen the mockery it was. But the lowering nameless horrors had pried him loose from that comforting world of landscaped reality, pitchforked him into this desolate wilderness where widdershins of madness clawed at him. And he thought he knew why.

'It's all that cursed gymnastic exercise,' he moaned. 'They did all that experimentation with rats and proved that unwanted exercise was more harmful than sitting still. Stress situations were bound to arise. I and my fellows want to get back and hit the couch and take a trip – and instead they keep us exercising in the gym so we don't degenerate. When I get out of this – ' The next occurring thought shattered him. '*If I get out of this!*'

In the harsh sky above him black and dirty-white birds began to circle. He could sense their beady eyes fastening on their targets in his own eyes. He could feel the sharp prick of their beaks, the tearing stripping of their talons. He sobbed with self-pitying helplessness, and crawled on, the blood from his palms and knees streaking clumsily behind him, clotting on the desert floor.

His tongue seemed to have ballooned into a monstrous growth bloating out his mouth and cheeks. He could no longer speak. He could feel; he could feel as though every nerve had been excoriated and exposed.

This was what the son of man must endure. This was what he must, in enduring, desire. This was what he must overcome.

He fell through the earth. The sensation, in hallucination, was familiar. He fell to the centre of the earth. His colours – his colours! – flamed and crackled and vibrated about him. He felt the heat and beat of fire; he saw the glow and flow of flame. He held out his arm – and a girl with the face of an angel weeping moved towards him. Her massy hair, long and darkly lustrous, waved behind her like the veil of Osiris. She smiled with waxen resignation at him, trailing her left leg, its knee tucked in to the right knee. She saw him and she moved past him, hypnotic, compelling, demanding – demanding of him something he could not give for he did not know the language of the demand.

The flames crackled louder. They scorched. He felt a sharp and psychically damaging prick in his arm. He reacted; he rolled over, reaching out sluggishly with the other hand, trying to rub away that prick and its meanings.

In the instant of time he saw through rolling fogs and swirling vapours the figure of a man approaching. The man showed flat and ugly features, a blunt and porcine look about his muzzle, a foxy twist to his eyes. He laughed as he saw Sheldon. He laughed with ugly sadistic pleasure. In one over-large hand he grasped a knife, a long slender liver-seeking knife. Laughing, he tossed Sheldon its mate.

'Fight, Sheldon, or you die! Fight, and you die! Take your choice, for alternative you have none.'

Sheldon caught the knife. The man wore tight crimson trousers and yellow cummerbund; bare of chest and bare of feet he was ready to fight. Around his left forearm he had wound a long scarlet scarf. Sheldon still wore his stained worker's smock – that, alone, sure sign that his hallucination had not been working aright.

Urgency possessed both men. They circled like dogs, bristling. A quick glittering stabbing, a succession of fluid motions, and a streaking line of blood and fire scorched along Sheldon's ribs. He gasped. He felt the pain as he had felt the pain in the desert; the blood from his palms clogged the hilt of his knife. Pear-shaped flickerings of light and colour drenched his vision. He shook his head angrily and circled warily, bearing up with the knife, clanging as it clashed with the other.

'Fight, then, it is, Sheldon. But you will die less easily – '

The knife fighter taunted him. He essayed a smooth series of rips and slashes and stabs, pressing Sheldon back into the fumes rising all around. The ground beneath vanished in vapours and dun ochre fogs and their legs appeared amputated at the calves. They moved without sure footing and conscious at every moment of the abyss.

Again that whiplike caress left a long angry slice of blood along Sheldon's ribs. He had no need to be reminded; but: 'You know you *will* die, Sheldon, even though this is an hallucination? Die, you worker scum, *die*!'

The knife fighter pressed harder; his blade a silvery blood-flecked halo of destruction.

Sheldon tried to meet that attack. His arm still tingled to the prick of the needle. How much longer, for god's sake, how much longer?

His foot slipped and he staggered. The fighter's knife tickled along his ribs. Off balance, all Sheldon could do was drive his bunched left fist into the fighter's face. He felt a most extraordinary sense of satisfaction as he felt the squashing pulping of bone and flesh.

'You stupid swine! You will die now, Sheldon, in the utmost agonies! I promise you!'

The glittering knife blade swept upwards, checked, slashed down. Blood ran from Sheldon's lacerated chest. He yelled his agony and drove forward, his own blade a ram before him, driving insanely at the jeering figure of the fighter. Agilely, the man skipped aside, his face bloody and sweating; but his eyes coals of vengeance.

Sheldon had recognised him by now. His prowess with the knife might be true or not; in an hallucination all that mattered was the effect on the hallucinated. This man – who was already dead with a knife in his chest – could reap a sardonic revenge with a knife out of the subconscious of his murderer. . . .

Sweating, shaking, his legs like toffee, Sheldon struggled away from another slashing forcing attack. He held the knife as prescribed for knife-fighting. He fought to stay alive. Blood stank. It smoked fumingly, thick and shining and dark, on their chests and arms and faces, dulling the sheen of the knives with a more awful glaze.

He had killed his man before this; he would do so again.

He waited for the next sure-footed attack; the man seemed to have no fear of where he trod, no sinking sensation of the ground falling away from his feet. He waited and then, as the knife swept in, he caught the man's wrist with the intention of disarming him. The knife-fighter knew that one. He turned his arm over and the blade of his knife licked along Sheldon's forearm like the tongue of a cat. Sheldon let go – fast – and leaped back.

The knife-fighter bared his teeth. He advanced again, crouched over, his face leering, shot with vicious enjoyment. His tongue touched his lips with furtive pleasure. He moved in. He kept on moving in.

Sheldon lifted his knife high. He snapped his hand back and then, as though he were going to throw, swung his shoulder forward.

The knife-fighter could believe, Sheldon hoped, that a man might throw a knife in such a fight as this. He would know Sheldon to be desperate. He ducked. His lithe body sagged sideways in instinctive reflex from the flung knife.

Instead, Sheldon leaped. Instead of hurling the knife, he hurled himself.

His blade sliced into the knife-fighter's stomach. It went in and in – close up to it, Sheldon saw the blade going in and in as though in exaggerated slow-motion. He saw the blood begin to spurt out. He thrust again, for the last time, hard and savagely, the cold steel bathed in crimson, opening its own mouth in flesh.

If the knife-fighter screamed, Sheldon did not know.

All sounds and sensations flickered, as though seen waveringly through a shimmer of interpenetrating squares and lozenges of green and brown and ochre, swaying with the wind of change, transitional.

He opened his eyes and stared up at Griselda.

The Horrible Truth had struck again.

When Sturm had chosen Archbold as his chief executive in the handling of insurance cases, he had been well aware of the cindery evil of the man, the emery-paper attitude not only to everyone else but to itself. No one liked anybody else in the world today; that made sound common sense; but for John Archbold dislike extended to inanimate objects – and to himself.

The man's thin, high-nosed face with the sallow swallowtailed marks down the cheeks, the prominent Adam's-apple, the limp and scanty hair, all contrived to suggest a worm gnawing a corpse.

John Archbold took almost as much pleasure from hazing workers as he took from a trip.

With a forced squad of Uppers recruited to handle tricky assurance cases, he strode across the workers' city. Sturm had given him his orders. 'Turn over a few worker cliques, rough them up a little – you might find something.'

He had already tumbled out three cliques, shivering men and women huddled on to the harsh concrete, their bleared faces and tousled hair softly out-of-place in the hard sunlight of the street. For the traps and alarms he had only contempt.

'They might stop a cretinous worker; never an Upper.'

He walked among them, this thin man with the tight leather boots against which he cracked a supple whip, walked with the stalking arrogance of a man who has found no personal dogma beyond that of a personal devil.

'Over there, Hanson,' he directed the bulldog-jawed assistant. 'That crumbled block looks promising. And it's still within a reasonable distance of the place of the murder. Get the lead outta your boots! Get moving!'

Hanson, dull and phlegmatic and thinking only of his next trip, moved solidly off, taking with him the other Uppers, all resenting this tearing away of reality to traipse about in the workers' city. Only Revenuers and the utterly dedicated really cared for slumming.

The teams Sturm had out looking for Vincent hated what they were doing as much as these Uppers detested this kind of work. The Insurance Assessors were a dying breed. No one bothered over much about revenge when the deed had been done and it wasn't you who lay with your throat cut. The deterrent values had been set and defined long since; now they tended to continue under the weight of their own momentum. Life, in workers' city and Upper city, was running down.

The sloppy tenement showed gap-teeth windows, blind eyes chancred over with decay, mumbling mouths forgetful of function. The Uppers kicked aside the naïve traps of the stairs, their electronic equipment beeping to trace the rudimentary alarm systems. With no caution but with much contempt, the Uppers ransacked the building.

'They were claiming that the class system had collapsed, back before the age of Material Plenty,' Archbold said with a flat joyless vehemence. 'High Tory politicians used to claim that the "working class" was an obsolete term. Only in the sense that the so-called working class did not, by and large, do much work, justified such a wilfully blind and selfish statement. What they wanted to call the lower orders was the "ignorant classes" or the "stupid classes" because they either could not or would not make the efforts necessary to bring them into the upper reaches of class. You cannot force a cloth-capped blue-collar man to walk bareheaded with a white-collar if he doesn't want to or can't. But you don't do him a favour by suggesting that, miraculously, his whole working class background means nothing.'

'They're in here,' Hanson shouted down. 'Pigging it in filth.'

'Workers,' said Archbold, with disgust. 'Sometimes one wonders if Joy Juice is worth them.'

'You try taking it away – ' began Hanson. Archbold looked at him. Hanson stopped short, licked his lips.

One of the old crones was given a sticking of the revivifying needle and then, reluctant to touch the workers, the Uppers left her to revive the others. 'Just like a foul den of autistic kids,' said Archbold, with immense finicky distaste.

The room's occupants, grunting and wheezing, pawing their eyes and mumbling, lifting their heads and swallowing re-

111

peatedly in the typically post-trip re-orientation, slowly came back from their realities to the world of reality.

The Horrible Truth had struck.

Zack Conrad could not meet the look he knew he would find in Dirk Havergen's eyes. They walked apart down the concrete walkway, seven stories up over the Avenue of Spheres, the anodised railings chipped and corroded in a serrated band on either hand. Corrosion ate at Conrad. He had picked himself up and walked away from the Revenue men, forgetting his desires to see the blood and the agony of the orange-faced leader, thinking only of the last insult offered him – him! – by that baboon-faced black-shirted hulk of faeces. There were two more worker knives. One for Havergen. One for baboon-face.

Yes.

Reve*noo* biz.

Revenge biz, too, reve*nooer*.

'There's a sign down there, Zack.' Havergen had been oddly complaisant since that undignified sprawl of Conrad's, almost as though, impossible though the concept could be, he felt a sharing of Conrad's experience.

'Yeah. That'll make the third since – ' Conrad mentally cuffed himself. Three since his humiliation. Angrily, he stumped down a winding once-ornate stairway between the faceless slabs of masonry on either hand. Huge blocks of matter, the building rose up and up, the end walls, supporting curtain walls, blank and unresponsive, echo-breeding. They formed a slot between them, a long-forgotten demarcation property-line, shaving off a space of air between enclosed stasis. The stairs ran down into the slot, reached the ground. Havergen jumped the last five steps lightly. Deliberately, Conrad placed his feet on the last step, stood a moment, looking along the alley.

The sign said:

GUZTAV LAWLOR
HIS LUXURY RELAX PALACE
CATERS ONLY FOR YOU

He remembered.

He sniggered out of his misery. 'Sturm will be pleased,' he said, cryptically to Havergen. 'We didn't miss a single one.'

'Well, of course not,' Havergen said tartly, striding off. He had, though, Conrad saw with an amused leer, loosened his gun in its holster. Conrad did not wish to experience a newdism with Havergen; but he sensed that the fat man had much in common with himself.

Lawlor's place at once showed itself in a different class from the other tripjoints scattered around in convenient water-tight hovels in the district. That ward, the Mary Roberts it had been, had struck a chill into Conrad. They were the real deadbeats in there. The real refuse, bumming a fix off anybody, doing whatever they could, trying to re-establish themselves in the ranks of the full-time workers and only occasionally succeeding. Here, in Lawlor's Relax Palace, the fixtures catered for the highest stratum of worker.

'Lawlor himself, now, must have a nerve,' said Havergen sarcastically. 'Giving himself airs, isn't he?'

'You mean the double-barrelled name? Well – some fool worker might believe Lawlor to be a defrocked Upper. Give him panache, an aura, that way. Cheap.'

'I'm promising myself I'm going to kick him in the teeth for his presumption, though,' Havergen said, promising himself with obvious relish.

'Sure.' Conrad couldn't care about that. His own mouth still stung. He had a great deal to remember. Oh, baboon-face, your number is up! Your race is run! Your chips are down! You have had it! You are going to be done, frizzled, fried and buried! Oh, yes, baboon-face . . .

'All right, Zack?' asked Havergen.

'Of course. Let's go in. Business seems quiet.' Up and down that slot he had last seen in darkness his scanner showed no sign of rising heat levels. Together, but not touching, they went into Guztav Lawlor's Palace.

Griselda whined in terror, her lips chafing over each other, her face a sagging sack of lines and wrinkles.

Sheldon sat up queasily. His body stung in weals of fire. He looked down. His smock was unripped and unslashed, save for the usual frayed edges. No blood dripped thick and clogging. He inspected his chest and ribs. White weals extended where the hallucinatory knife had sliced. Yes. He'd been lucky. He felt as though he'd been in a knife fight; the smell of sweat and fear and blood still enmeshed him; but he was alive still, ready after a fashion to go back on shift and then to return to the couch and a trip – Something not as it should be struck him about the thought; but before he could collect himself a sandpapery voice rasped in his ear.

'Get downstairs! Move! Pick it hup, you pile of filth!'

Dazed, he looked up.

Human voice had waked him and now he drowned in them.

A hand gripped the collar of his smock, twisted, constricted, flung him forcefully face-down.

'Get on, get on!' Another hand pushed, a boot kicked, he sprawled, catching his ear hard against the leg of a couch. He swallowed convulsively, scrabbled up, tried to stand and was again shrewdly kicked and knocked staggering.

His non-existent psychosomatic wounds burned like arteries of acid. He felt sick. He pulled himself up again, trying to clear the fog in his head, trying to see what was going on – a raid? It must be, a raid.

He made a low sound in his throat, a furry bestiality of anger. A hand pushed him and he reeled to the door. Another unseen hand cuffed him on and he tripped to fall shapelessly down the harsh concrete stairs. His lip kissed the concrete and split and he tasted real blood, alive and thick and salty.

Booted, manhandled and hazed, he reeled out into the street.

Some of the others of his clique huddled there like abandoned luggage. Duboys and Patti and Thomasina, quaking. Deedee with her eyes so large and frightened she looked like a wombat toy. Griselda squashed down beside Sheldon, shaking all over like a cellophane bag filled with water. The dark-haired girl of his imagination shumbled down the stairs and span out into the street, her dark hair a sombre halo as she whirled. Somehow Sheldon slobbered to his feet and caught her in his arms, cradled her.

'No, no!' she sobbed, fighting him with stiff arms.

'It's me,' he said. He shared her fear so completely he could give no comfort. They huddled on the ground together, arms about each other, unable to go on in their imagination to what lay ahead.

Archbold strutted down the stairs to survey his prizes.

'What a miserable bunch of drop-outs,' he said, some flickering spark of baleful humour stirring him darkly. 'By the light of LSD,' he swore with the old blasphemy, 'they'll make a nice Joy-Juice bonfire. Take 'em away!'

Dark against the mid-day sunlight the workers filed away, silently.

'This is real, isn't it?' whispered Minch.

'Yes – I think so.' Sheldon remembered the last few moments of his hallucination. He remembered that blasphemous mouth, the deserts, the eyeless skulls, the knife fight. He writhed. 'Something went – wrong – with my trip,' he said, reluctantly, communicating something beyond the mere trivialities of everyday convenience.

'You, too?' Minch hobbled along at his side. Without realising he had done it until he felt her waist warm and slender in his grasp, he put an arm about her to help her along.

'That's not the first – ' He swallowed. 'I mean – I've had – funny – trips before. A bit – *off*.'

'So've I. Nasty.'

They talked perfectly naturally about their trips in their present situation; for that was mere reality of the real world, thin and insubstantial beside the infinitely more rewarding reality of their minds.

Minch did say, falteringly: 'Where are we going?' To which, half-angry and half-frightened, Sheldon replied: 'I've no idea. But I've a needle and a couple of packets of good stuff – no dirt – in my pockets. We'll be all right for a bit.'

He groped around in his mind for the inner significance of that odd 'we'. He'd meant to say I'll be all right. But the we had – popped out. He looked along the street against mid-day glare falling between the ziggurats and striking back from the paving stones. Wherever they were going the Uppers knew what they were doing.

The march continued. Joined by workers from other routed-out cliques, they trailed disconsolately southwards. Like a mindless circling of beetles in the dust they crawled between those vast and decaying buildings whose rounded pompously confident fronts rounded now on emptiness.

Archbold stopped off by the flier. Not for him the long dusty walk back. Hanson, with his bulldog tenacity, would be the man for that.

The radio hissed with a pathetic attempt to regain the days when the wavebands were filled with the idle chatter of a garrulous world. 'Sturm?' Called out Archbold, his desiccated face shadowed and highlighted like granite cliffs. We've rounded up twenty-five or thirty. Will that be enough?'

Sturm's voice growled down the static. 'Yes. Bring them in. The Revenuers report another disconnection – a dump called The Unending Bliss – we'll unend 'em all right.' Dutifully, Archbold sniggered. 'We'll milk them dry! Tony Lawrence's death and these deliberate evasions of revenue are connected. Who the hell do these dumb workers think they are, anyway?'

'Be right with you,' and Archbold cut the connection.

Ambiguity and anonymous Kafka-like controls for workers had proved in the past of expected efficacy; but nothing ever remained static, least of all a crumbling city and civilisation. If ever anyone thought that then they had not thought enough. Movement paced and pulsed through birth, growth and decay. Even death proved only to be the ultimate movement.

Archbold swung himself into the flier, snapped a curt order at the driver, and shot ahead of the trudging fodder below towards the shining southern Upper city.

10

His three assistants grasping the man now called Jones-Smith (or Smith-Jones) the man in the white coat unhurriedly brought his hypodermic needle forward. S-J struggled. He wrenched his arms up and down, twisting his wrists, feeling the ease with which these hallucinations constricted him. The end of the needle glinted sparkily. A jet of green liquid ejaculated. Smith-Jones stopped struggling.

He had been Wendell, and Higham, and Dobel, and Commer, and Smith and Jones – and how many others in between he could not now remember. The time had come once more for him to move on.

And still the leopard woman had not glided into this manifestation.

He did not hesitate. 'I will,' he said, loudly and with firm authority, 'I will be Robinson.'

As he said it, as the words formed on his lips and moved his tongue, he realised what this man in the white coat had done to him – for he had entered this hallucination as Jones, with determination – and the white-coated man had called him Smith. And the name had stuck, had double-barrelled, he was J-S or S-J – and he was still in this hallucination. He was still here. The man in the white coat advanced towards him with the needle held ready for the stinging plunge. The assistants grasped him tightly.

'I am Robinson!' he shouted with animal despair.

'Hold still, Robinson,' snarled one of the assistants. 'I'll break your arm off if you struggle!'

He recognised with disgust that the attitude of the assistants reflected a growing diathesis of callous behaviourism inseparable from mental treatments. Inseparable but not inevitable, he might like to believe; but at this moment, trapped in a hallucination with deep-surgery, madness or disfigurement awaiting him, he could feel now only the profound bowel-movements of despair.

His struggles resembled those of a bird caught in a trap.

For the moment from exhaustion and fear he had remained limp. Infinitesimally the clenching hands on his arms slackened. Instantly, like a youth leaping the white-hot coals, he sprang free.

Head down, feet pumping, he charged for the exit.

'Catch him!' and 'After him!' rang out buglingly.

The exit gave on to a narrow rutted ochre road, winding entrenched, overcast with a uniform grey pall, a leprous sky with the blasphemous beauty of high-explosive flowers blossoming with red detritus on every side. Robinson ducked his head as the shrapnel whizzed by. After him the assistants and the man in the white coat stumbled and rebounded down the trench, leaping the decomposing bodies of dead men, kicking severed heads, clanging against abandoned mess-tins, rifles, gasmasks and skinless skulls.

Robinson fell. For all his badminton his body had not retained the cunning sinew and nerve of youth. He fell, gasping, mud and faeces bubbling from the faucets of breath of his nostrils and mouth.

They lifted him. They took him back, holding him like one who is intent on his self-destruction.

Mud dripped from his clothes, the white nylon shirt and dark slacks given him so long ago by Comfort's red-headed courtesans. Oh for the days of yester-hallucic! The days of happy aspirations when what he decided was to happen happened. Upside down, head hanging, eyeballs showing more white than colour, he was whisked back through the door and up a side corridor into the sterile horror of the operating theatre.

Flung on the table whose chromium surfaces leered at him with reflected terror, he lay like an animal in a zoo cage trembling and trapped and traumatic.

He made one last effort.

'My name is Sebastien Lazade von Bochstein dos Santos y Circumvillion Hugglewhite! And I command you to begone!'

The man in the white coat laid a doughy warm hand on his forehead. 'There, there, lad. You'll soon be all right. You narcotics bums are all alike; want everything for nothing from this world. Well – ' The man's teeth were unmannerly white, with a gold filling flashing. 'We'll soon sort you out.'

The assistants sniggered.

'Go away!' screamed Robinson (etc.). *'Go away!'*

Unlike the figments of a dream, the symbols of his hallucinated mind remained four square and concrete in their reality.

The man in the white coat bent over him. The hypodermic needle looked the size of a vacuum cleaner.

The assistants swung over solid steel clamps, hollowed to fit over his biceps and thighs. They *thunkked* as they slammed into position. Robinson heard the sliding clicks of bolts thrust home. He could not move. His head was clasped between leather and plastic pads as though gripped between the thighs of a wrestler.

'What are you going to do?' he gasped, his lips stiff and protruding, his neck aching, his eyes stinging.

The vacuum cleaner nozzle waved airily. 'I'm just going to put you under. Then we're trepanning – '

'Not a prefontal! Please – !'

'Oh, no!' The man in the white coat glanced for flattering approval from his assistants. 'Oh dearie me, no. No pre-frontal lobotomy for you.' He chuckled with immense satisfaction.

'No. . . ?'

'Of course not! We're removing the entire brain!' and he drove the needle home.

Contact.

Trees.

Trees?

Anachronisms. All rooted-out. Chlorophyll for the mouth, never for leaves. Trees – ha, ha, ha, ha, ha-aah!

He stood on the edge of an abandoned orbital-vehicle bomber base. Beyond the thin and ragged edge of trees the hangars, fallen in, disused, decrepit and dusty, rose like forgotten forms from primeval swamps. A wind blew detritus about his legs; leaves, papers, scraps from log-books charting unmade flights beyond the stratosphere, a woman's scarf. Unthinkingly he bent and picked the scarf from its scattering of refuse.

Cerise and blatant, it fitted the mood of all the things this orbital-vehicle bomber base had never been.

No H-bombs had been dropped by those collapsing bombers within the sheds. No man had agonised over his part in social genocide. No residue of guilt had patterned the shape of fifty years.

He looked about him. The man in the white coat was not here, that was self-evident. Neither were his sadistic assistants. One, he remembered, had dribbled continuously down a badly-shaven chin. They were gone.

But where was he?

He began to walk away from the abandoned bomber base, looking for a clue to existence. Somewhere in his mind a small clock ticked away at the thought: 'When I get my hands on Lawlor I'll wring his neck!'

The thought had little power to comfort him, locked within a hallucinatory experience within a hallucination within. . . . He had no idea how far down he had gone.

Like the return from synthetic cubism which opened the gates to abstractionism, this journey the man in the white coat had sent him on must lead to a further revelation, a further and more profound pushing back of the frontiers between the mysticism of life and the reality that true life negated. How much longer he must go on, how much longer he must suffer, he could not tell. If only he could clearly recall just what he had told Lawlor, or Lawlor's computer, to do, he would feel that he was not walking blindly into a never-ending tunnel, bottled and corked for eternity.

A road formed beneath his feet and when the red convertible pulled up, the wild beat of music like a fauve conception done in sound drumming and twanging from the radio, he felt not the slightest surprise. The girl leaned towards him, displaying artful Euclidean geometry.

'Yes?' she said, lifting one pale lip.

'Yes,' he answered, getting in.

They drove to the jetty. Sail boats, yachts, speedboats, motor launches, lay swaying on the water. The horizon, beneath a flat and universally negative blue, placed a bold bar across vision.

Sunlight burned on the water, like burred bronze edges. They went down to the speedboat.

Coiled pipeclayed ropes. Winking brass. Tanned teak. The fuel-cell motive power combined hydrogen and oxygen to produce electricity, with water as a by-product. The girl with the disfigured face stepped in, halting with one leg bent, her halter dress and white shoes splashes of brilliance against the green of plastic seating.

'I'll drive,' she said. Her hair a flame of gold under the sun they sped in a saucer of creaming water out past the bobbing lines of anchored craft.

Water hit the keel of the speedboat with massive bludgeons, solid and rhythmical, bounce and soar, bounce and soar. Robinson glanced covertly at the girl, seeing the dusting of fine gold hairs over her lip, the firmness of her jaw, faintly waxy and ripe. Water slopped inboard. He ignored it. The boat curved steeply, like a stone it skimmed the wave crests, then settled as the girl cut the power. The speedboat wallowed.

A sailboat puffed towards them, a white triangular finger against the intolerable blue glare of the sky.

In the fibre-glass sail-dinghy a man with a cadaverous face, with hollow eyes and a weak mouth, sat idly lifting two mirrors, into one of which he would peer with an intent down-drawn consciously serious look. Then he would look into the other mirror as though hoping to find the same reflection there.

A child's bucket of sand stood at his elbow. On the sand lay a heap of drying crystals. In the bows of the boat a tailor's dummy, a fashion model, had been dropped. The dummy's plastic waist thinned to near invisibility, the breasts swelled in plastic profusion. It wore a couple of X-ray plates haphazardly over one shoulder.

Robinson felt only nausea.

'Be kinder,' the girl said, her face calm and without discernible feeling.

'Kind?' said Robinson with despair. 'I believe I know what has been happening and I am frightened.'

'That man in the sailing dinghy. He was frightened. Now all he can do is compose dubious stories in a cryptic language of his own in order to persuade the woman he had seduced to pose for obscene photographs.'

121

'Poor devil,' said Robinson. Then he laughed with a harsh wracking self-pitying mirth. 'Why do I feel sorry for a figment of my own hallucinations? I am the one to feel sorrow for myself. I know who I am – *I do know!*'

The sea dried up. One moment they were rocking gently in the speedboat watching a maniac watching his mirrors; the next they lay canted on drying sand with steam rising about them and fishes flopping everywhere like corn on a griddle.

'The ancient scars,' said Robinson, on a breath, 'have been glorified, it seems, and the titanic tears have dried.'

'But,' the girl said gently. 'But this is not the last sea nor are there the hapless stars.' Her figure began to fade. The idiot in the sail dinghy had long since been forgotten. The sand dried and cracked into mud. The speedboat collapsed with a little sigh. A tiny wind lifted soft shreds of wood.

'Don't go – ' called Robinson.

'Goodbyee-ee – '

He stood alone encompassed by a crazy-paving of cracked mud, as far as he could see, out of sight around the horizon's rim.

Limply, he waited. Wendell, Higham, Dobel, Commer, Smith, Jones and Robinson. All of them vacuous, all proving beyond reasonable doubt what he now saw to be the answer – and that answer in its turn brought fresh problems.

The changing of names meant nothing. That had been a whim. He could have been any name at all throughout. The fault lay in himself, in the very core of his being human, ironically so, and he himself had produced these hideous results.

Limply, he waited.

The sun melted and dripped down the sky. Fleetingly he was reminded of the moment he had stood on a narrow plank above the balefires of a vast host and watched the tears of colour cascade down the sky. He hoped for the interpenetrating blue and green and brown squares to come vibrating up before the screen of his mind; but he knew that hope to be vain.

Limply, he waited.

The vast cracked landscape around him, like unending haphazard rows of mud saucers, separated by wide bottomless chasms, moved with a long low subterranean surge. A few puffs of vapour rose from the black rifts. The man in the white coat

122

had pricked him with the needle some time ago and this waiting sawed away at Robinson (also) and caused him to turn his head round and about, uneasily, as though at any minute in this desolate landscape the leopard woman would glide mincingly towards him. She might. Now he could no longer guarantee what his mind would do.

The sky split.

Limply, he waited.

The sky split and light spilled down and a face as large as a dirigible floated there, tombstone teeth clicking, cerise lips slipping past them, grimacing. A voice said with eerie overtones and feedbacks and echoes: 'He's coming around.'

Another voice said: 'And about time, too.'

Where?

Real terror flattened his stomach muscles, closed his throat, stretched his facial muscles into a rictus of terror. A roaring buzz saw inside his head, lights flashing in his eyes, the feeling of stopping heart and blocked arteries and collapsing lungs, the deliquescence of the human spirit assaulted and insulted him and rendered him of insignificant impotence.

'Hold up!' The voice still echoed and re-echoed. 'Grab his arms.'

He waited for the feel of the solid steel straps, the plastic head pads . . .

He was hauled and pulled up to sit on the couch.

Couch.

He blinked his eyes which had filled with moisture. A hand passed him a tissue. He wiped his eyes and blew his nose. He could feel the couch, he could half-see the floor and a pair of plastic-leather shoes and dark green slacks. His shirt, too, was dark green. Not a white nylon shirt, not grey slacks, not slippers.

The stranding tissues of hallucination had torn.

Firmly, he stood up. He looked about. 'The 'Orrible Troof!' he said, and shivered, and laughed suddenly.

'We used a revivifying needle. We had to.'

'Why?'

In that single monosyllable he had regained perfect control of himself. He moved away from the couch with its tumbled sweat-stained sheets. Further down the small lounge three other men and a girl lay enwrapped in their private inscapes.

Workers, they came of a caste within the worker hierarchy that habitually demanded luxury in the inessentials of life as some small recompense for the lives they had lost. One of these days, he promised himself, he'd penetrate right down into the most abandoned of worker tripjoints, find out what went on there.

'Where's Lawlor?' he growled at the two young men who had roused him. They were, he saw at a single glance, typical products of the Upper closed-city. Scared as all hell to be out with only the sky for roof.

'We have him under arrest, Vincent. Sturm is very disturbed by these disconnection incidents –'

'There are more? What's your name, anyway?'

'I am Zack Conrad,' the younger man said, with a stiff flash of pride. He indicated the other. 'This is Gerard McBain. We've had a time finding you.'

'Tell me.'

'Workers are disconnecting the Joy Juice effluvia emanations. Workers are complaining about their drug qualities. One government drug store was raided and set alight. We –' Conrad licked his lips. He would *not* think of the first cupboard by the door. 'We seem to be facing a – revolution – Sturm called it.'

'That won't get far. No work, no drugs, no hallucinofabs.'

'Yes, but –'

'But what, boy!'

'Sturm wants you to report to him right away.'

'I'll report to Sturm when I know what *to* report, boy!'

'Yes, Vincent, certainly.'

'Bring Lawlor in here. Pronto!'

'Yes.' Conrad stared at McBain. He looked enough like Tony Lawrence or Dirk Havergen to make that marginally interesting. 'Get Lawlor in here, Gerard – fast!'

When three of Archbold's bully boys brought Lawlor in, the little worker tripjoint proprietor's face wore a puzzled, lax, swivelling expression, as though he had just been struck by a swing door. He didn't appear frightened.

'I gave you your instructions, Lawlor,' said Vincent, thrusting his mass of beard out, swelling himself up with the deliberate bullying of a frog. 'What have you been up to, hey?'

'Nuffing. I know nothing at all whatsoever completely innocent simon pure of what they say. It wasn't me. I've been on a

124

trip same as you – ' His vacuous face with its blackcurrant-like eyes now steamed into overlarge bewilderment expressed absolute non-comprehension.

Vincent thought of his own trip: of the sinking sensation of being made to look small, of the leopard woman, of the man in the white coat, of all the incidents that had teemed within his skull.

Lawlor said: 'I didn't disconnect.'

'That doesn't concern me. You'll answer for that to the Inland Revenue.'

Zack Conrad looked his surprise; after a quick grimace he hid that expression. Havergen gone; baboon-face to go.

Vincent knew, now, what ailed reality. But he must as the last reputable scientist make sure. He must sweep away any other cause before he presented Sturm with his findings. 'You and I, Lawlor,' he said with soft and tiger-clawing emphasis, 'are going to inspect every inch of your equipment, to inspect all your stock of drugs, to strip down every hallucinofab. If there is an adulterant I shall find it – although I know there is not.' He glowered around on Conrad and McBain. 'You two know nothing of science, so go and get lost!'

'Yes, Vincent,' they said, dutifully, quickly.

As he excited from Guztav Lawlor's Luxury Relax Palace, Zack Conrad, whose face expressed only bored indifference and impatient longing for his next trip, allowed himself one single luxurious glance at the cupboard by the door.

In there, with blood choking him and a worker's knife in his back, Dirk Havergen would never again have the chance of spitting at Zack Conrad.

Conrad felt the last knife. Baboon-face would make a tasty chaser.

McBain said, nervously: 'Is it safe out there, Zack?'

Casually, Conrad lifted the scanner. 'There are plenty of heat levels rising,' he said laconically. 'But they're mostly from Uppers chasing workers. If the workers wish to be silly, I'm sure we can accommodate them.'

McBain swallowed. 'I had a rotten last trip!' he burst out, shamefacedly, as though owning to heterosexuality in Sodom. 'It didn't go – right.'

Conrad stared at him. 'Me, too,' he said, shortly. Then: 'But I don't talk about it.'

'No.'

'Aithough — ' He stepped out with a final look at the cupboard from which shortly a thin red stream should flow. 'Although I hope Vincent can do something quickly. I wouldn't like another trip like my last.'

The deep diapason of praise swelled loudly in his ears.

'Vive l'Empereur!' crashed shrilly from the long ranks of tall, bearskinned, moustached Old Guard.

'Banzai! Banzai!' frothed frenetically from the massed squadrons of Kamikaze pilots, the Kempetai solidly behind them.

'Morituri te salutimus!' barked fatalistically from the armoured, naked, gladius-waving, net-coiling gladiators and retiarii on the bloodiest sands.

The solidly packed masses, black-clad, brown-clad, extending in a madman's perspective before him beneath the pendulous banners, right arms gauntly upraised, chanted again and again: 'Sieg Heil! Sieg Heil! Heil Sturm! *Heil Sturm!* HEIL STURM!'

Sturm smiled and it was good.

A negligent hand waved and he stood on the bridge of a battleship driving her purposeful way through the waves, fifty thousand tons displacement thrumming forward with the full power of one hundred and fifty thousand horses, spume lofting to fall short of his airy perch. 'You may open fire, admiral — '

Eight fifteen-inch guns bellowing their brown cottonwool, battering nineteen hundred and twenty pounds of steel, copper and lyddite over the horizon. The grim confident wait — sudden death would now be swooping from the skies over there on the hostile fleet.

A tall white spuming spectre, rising from the sea hard on the starboard bow. Another chasmed seaquake and the high toppling loft of white water. A third . . . The shudder of the ship, the shake of metal, the crashing smashing of the air about his ears. Smoke and flame and pain. The ship struggling, mortally wounded. The fire forking down, spreading, consuming cordite trays, lancing impishly through cordite magazines, shell magazines, uprooting the capital ship like a tree wrenched from the earth, broken, bleeding, shattered.

Water in his mouth, fire in his nostrils . . .

Sturm screamed.

He struggled and writhed.

He thrashed about as though hooked and fluked on a whaler's harpoon, sea-coaming, blood-spattering, weakening.

He opened his eyes and stared up. His hands had clenched so that the nails half-mooned his palms.

His face dripped sweat.

Above his head a glass ceiling showed an angle of his room. Seeing that famous smile, half-lit for him alone, he sank back on the couch, breathing hardly still; but reassured. From hallucinated reality he was back to un-hallucinated reality.

From the low sandalwood table beside the couch he took a small ivory box, carved and shone with use, and withdrew two pills, swallowing these dry and very expertly. He felt a little better at once.

Well?

What?

What on this earth . . .?

'Where the raving hell's Vincent?' he grumbled aloud, and stood up, without a tremor, automatically flexing muscles, rippling his skin, pulling and pushing himself back into top physical condition.

Something very serious was wrong. Not for the first time lately had he experienced an unpleasant twist to his trips. Others had mentioned it. Old Faller, over at the Faller Insurance Tower, had died of it, never awaking from his last trip. Sturm had no reason to suppose he had been assassinated, although six months ago that would have been the immediate explanation for the death. Now – now all hell was breaking out on the hallucination level of life. Faller had died presumably because he had experienced an unpleasant trip. It happened occasionally; now it was happening with such frequency that –

But that, of course, was impossible – unthinkable.

For an Upper, now, only one thing remained for Sturm to do. Like all Uppers, he made a ceremony of it; but, being Sturm, he could indulge whenever he wished.

This room – square, low-ceilinged, walled in lime-green and grey, the floor smothered in nut-brown carpets and ivory rugs, the long low furniture cane and foam, unobtrusive, the lights globular and orange – soothed him and nerved him pleasantly. He de-polarised the glass and shut himself into his own cocoon within the greater cocoon of the room. He passed by the telescope mounted in the angle of polarised windows, giving the gleaming brass a light affecionate pat, remembering happy hours spent viewing his treasures out there in the hangar.

The red lacquer cabinet opened with an elaborate psychic key. Inside, on shallow shelves, lay revealed the accumulators, the condensers, like master delay lines, ranked for his use. Musing, reading the labels, he selected the newest, rawest, toughest worker he could find from the catalogue. Just at the moment he felt in no mood for the softer, muskier, more plangent girls with which the cabinet was mostly provided.

He took the jar of blued glass from the shelf and, holding it in both hands, walked back to a low lounging chair before a three-legged stool. He placed the blue jar down carefully on the stool, arranging it geometrically at the centre of the angles of the triangle. Then he sank back on his heels and for a moment contemplated the light striking down on the curved blue glass, its dusting of silver decomposition giving it the look of Roman glass discovered after two thousand years.

When his breathing had steadied, when his eyes saw clearly, when his wrists had ceased to pain, he moved with dutiful humility towards the stool. He picked up the jar. He felt its cool roundness, the faintly greasy slick to it, the reassurance it gave.

Some Uppers carried this ritual through as though they inhabited a medical school or a scientific laboratory, all white coats and test tubes and bubbling retorts, with bus bars crackling from overload. That was their privilege.

For Sturm, meticulous, domineering, ruthless, the imbibing of Joy Juice fell into a more personal, less cold, less synthetic frame. He rejected his own image. For this and this alone he became less than Sturm; and in that simple act knew he became greater than Sturm. For Joy Juice made everything that was Sturm possible.

In a disintergrating society, with the hope of prolifes to prevent fatal decay of the body, with isolation and suspicion the natural lot of all mankind, the prolongation of the human span might appear ludicrous. No man who had lived with hope, no man who had lived with joy, no man who had lived to conquer sorrow could share that view. The life of a man was his most precious possession. To enlarge it he might do – oh, any of the things Sturm and the Uppers had done.

The life of the spirit had been engulfed, subsumed and incarcerated in the life of hallucination. Sturm had omitted spiritual matters from his methods. He remembered God, he knew that most of the churches still stood and were used as convenient places to sling a hammock in lieu of a tripjoint; but for Sturm and his Uppers, for the Uppers of the city and of the world, extension of life through Joy Juice had imperceptibly and yet inevitably grown into life with and for Joy Juice.

He completed his devotions before the mystic blue jar.

He took up the little – so simple! – apparatus of leads and temple-pads. He slipped the spring over his head and adjusted the pads comfortably over his temples. He thrust the leads down into the leads embedded in the cork seal of the bottle. Plastic cork, of course. He sat back, at ease, almost slouching, eyes half-closed, mouth half-open, drinking in the life spirit.

The life spirit poured into him, raw and smoky and primeval, running through his central nervous system, rilling out through all his being, recharging exhausted cells, strengthening lax fibres, firming his whole physical frame. He gave small crooning sounds of pleasure. He felt the body and being that was Adolf Eric Sturm growing and recuperating, flowering and enlarging.

When the jar was empty he still sat for a few moments, reliving in shivery memory the sensuous impressions of fulfilment.

Then, briskly, he detached the leads, put away the apparatus and pitched the jar down the waste chute where it would go to central despatch to be re-filled with the life spirit drained off from another worker in drugged sleep.

'If those damned workers think we'll supply them with drugs if they disconnect the Joy Juice leads, then they're hypnomanic!' Sturm said with jovial viciousness, knowing that with the drugs of hallucination under the Uppers' hands no one alive could gainsay them.

With the surety of many score years' life bubbling within him, he felt only contempt and rancour for the workers. 'I'll sort them out a saga apiece – and then cut them loose!' he said, and laughed. 'If I sewed up my father and mother in a saga I can damn well do anything I like at all – and no one in this city is going to stop me!'

11

As though the Passing Bells had tolled in a unison of fervour;
as though a damped down fire had sprung up simultaneously
in a thousand places; as though a virus had bred prolifically in
a single instant of virulence, all over the city workers
clamoured and rioted and ripped out Joy Juice connections,
refusing to work.

The burden of their complaints was universal and bitter.

'Our trips are going wrong! You Uppers – your drugs are
valueless and your lucimechs jangling toys! We believe these
connections you insist we make when we take a trip are causing
these hideous nightmares!'

Beneath the open sky of the old city a pall of gloom and
terror spread. A party of Uppers was ambushed and before
their spiteful guns could beat off the frenzied attack half a
dozen of them lay dead in their own blood. The knives of the
workers were sharp and quick.

Radios crackled as never before for a hundred years. Fliers
with grim-faced Revenue men descended in hovering hate.
Every electric car that would run was pressed into service on
wobbling tyres and protesting engines. The Joy Juice effluvia,
collected by the connections situated beneath every worker
couch, ran from thence along the old telephone wires veining
the city, concentrated at the collapsing telephone exchanges,
sent by coaxial cable direct to the processing vats of the
Uppers' city pharmacy. Now those wires were wantonly cut.
Underground cables were dug up and slashed with manic
ferocity.

No worker knew why the effluvia connections were made. He
knew only that if they were not made he would receive no

drugs, though he present all the discarded gold in the dust-infested vaults of Fort Knox.

But buried superstition, cast out with the rationality of the age of Material Plenty, remained no longer buried, refused to stay cast out. These sinister connections open-mouthed beneath every worker's head – what did they *do*? Why? They – it must be, it could only be! – they brought the hideous torment in place of sweet hallucics. Surely. They must – out with them! Rip and slash, follow up the wires, dig and fell, root out the evil at its source. Bring back the days of sweet and fanciful hallucination, when every young worker went to bed with the golden-haired girl of his dreams and every young worker-girl chose from among a throng of suitors, chose and discarded the balance . . .

The workers raged.

More time was spent by workers not working or exercising in the gym out of hallucination than had been known for over a century. Now mobs of workers infested the streets. And – even more sinisterly – they were not indiscriminately fighting among themselves, as they would previously have done. Any Upper sighted was the immediate signal for a wolf-like ferocious pack attack. But the workers were – a word that was near-obscene – were co-operating.

Tight-faced Uppers met. Insurance Companies that met only to haggle the price of a man's death now met in reluctant counter to the workers.

As Sturm put it: 'When any man is awake and active he uses up his life spirit to the full; but when he is asleep or hallucinated, he scarecely disturbs that deep source. So when we suck from a man – or a woman – the life spirit to bottle it in accumulators for our later use we are not depriving anyone of anything.'

Snortsen of Snortsen Insurance, growled: 'You're speaking wildly, Adolf.' He knuckled bristly white eyebrows and wheezed through plastic lungs. 'Who the hell cares about the workers? If they object to giving us their life spirit we'll take the Joy Juice from them all in a sewn up saga.'

'You can't have everyone in a saga!' objected Lejauen, of Lejauen Assurance. He rubbed gnarled hands together, wincing as his new heart picked up the beat from the rest of the profiles crammed into his chest cavity. 'If we could, we would.'

'We know the work the workers do is mostly fake, a sop to make them believe they are working – psychological tests are still coming in on that and I'm not convinced,' – Sturm glared about, bristly and square and hostile – 'not at all convinced of the need. However, we can put perhaps seventy five per cent into a sewn up saga. But you know the difficulties encountered with breeding – '

Snortsen coughed and one of his wives wiped his chin.

Sturm had chosen to meet the heads of the other Insurance Companies with his screens in a simple black room furnished only with a chair, in which he sat, the screens and the camera. The others might show all manner of distracting backgrounds when they met on closed circuit TV; Sturm had his standards. Old Washington, for instance, was already snoring on his couch, out on a trip. Sturm with a reluctance he felt for the very first time in his life did not envy Washington. Trips were becoming suddenly deadly.

And everyone was dry.

Looking around on the circle of screens now, with their faces fierce, or grim, or frightened, or plain bored, Sturm saw one dominant motif there, one overwhelming desire. All these men and women wished to get on to the couch and take a trip free from worry, away from the hideousness of this reality. In this, the Uppers shared the same fate as the workers.

Karen Oldenshaw of Oldenshaw Insurance, said tartly: 'Vincent is insured with your Company, Adolf. What are you doing? As the last reputable scientist who might understand these matters he is vital to us – you great fat pig!' she blazed at him in a return to normalcy. 'Why don't you get off your over-padded butt and find him?'

'He is being looked after, Karen, you scraggy hag,' Sturm said absently. His private hookup radio clamped to his ear said: 'This is Zack Conrad. We have found Vincent.' The voice carried its triumph clearly. 'He thinks he knows the answer to the problem – '

Sturm flicked off his microphone switch to his TV camera. 'Only thinks!' he rasped through his throat mike at Conrad. 'He keeps telling us he is the last of the only true and genuine scientists – a biochemist, psychologist and flaming dispensing physician all rolled into one – so let him come through with the proof! I want to know what's wrong with the drugs. And

133

the lucimechs. And you'd better tell Vincent – '

Something unusual for Sturm occurred then. An auditor switched off on him. He was left fuming down a dead mike, with stuffy blankness in his earphone.

The coincidence of the answer treading on the exhaust pipe of the question was no novelty to Sturm; all his life coincidence had worked hard for him, as it must for every successful man.

Karen Oldenshaw was saying with bitter down-drooping mouth and scornful eyes fixed on Sturm's lowering face: 'We're all sick of your high-and-mighty ways in the city, Adolf. Just because you have Vincent. Anyone can control semi-intelligent workers by bread and circuses – and we don't have to provide real circuses any more. Anyone of us can do all you can do and more. We, too, hand out drugs to the workers and give them the chance to explore inner landscapes – '

Sturm switched on the microphone. 'Inner landscapes?' he said with insolent authority. 'Oh – you mean inscapes.'

'Whatever the hell they are – we want to know why they're not working any more!'

'I have Vincent working on that problem right this minute. I've just had a call. No doubt I'll inform you of the answer as soon as I have it myself.' He leaned forward in that abrupt charging manner of his. 'In the meantime tell your Assessors and the Revenue men to clamp down on workers' city! Tell them to show no mercy! Once we have the answer the workers will come to heel – but until they do give them no single chance – not one!'

He switched off the camera and the clustered screens before the other Insurers had time to answer.

Just as well, decided Sturm then, just as bloody well he had never joined the government. That bunch of old should-be saga'd women were running around in diminishing ovals – the laws of Kepler applied to them, too. If not to us. He stood up, stretching, playing his muscles like an orchestra, wondering what he would do to Zack Conrad for switching off in the middle of a conversation.

His mind clicked along grooves. The trouble always was these youngsters felt their damp new-ex-chrysalis wings as giving them the dry maturity of experience. Conrad could be disciplined easily enough. Withdrawal of drugs whipped any man to heel. But this must in some way be tied up with the workers' revolt – for, stupid in reality though that concept must be, Sturm could not but help view the disturbances in that light. He fretted about that all the way to his telescope. He needed to spy out into his hangar, lacking the desire actually to walk out there in person, and look through his telescope at the wonders and beauties of the last and greatest art collection in the world. Doing that would give him calmness and precision with which to plan his next moves.

The luminous eye of the telescope picked out the white marble frozen-movement, all frenzy and passionate calm, of the Saint Agnes on the Pyre, by Ercole Ferrata. The statue lived of itself. Bernini's influence was felt as a turning movement of light. The pyre flamed coldly. The saint's eyes upturned with ecstatic longing, her martyrdom already conceived and over and the flames mere agents of an accepted fate.

Archbold called through on the radiophone.

At first Sturm wanted to brush him off; but as the man talked Sturm, devouring the statue, saw and understood what he meant. He smiled. 'Yes, John,' he said smoothly. 'I'll be right down.'

As Karen Oldenshaw said bitterly to old Snortsen: 'Everything depends on Adolf and Vincent, now – Sturm and Cheesman, between them, control everything – curse them!'

Guztav Lawlor's Luxury Relax Palace had been to all intents and purposes torn apart. Once it had been a cathedral, new and modishly gaunt of architecture, spanning the centuries of Early English and Perpendicular and Coventry and Liverpool. Lawlor had re-rigged it for lucimechs and drug-trips. As a tripjoint it had been first class. Now Vincent and his men had stripped it bare, ripping back the modern world's artifacts and exposing the original stone and glass and steel.

The cathedral now looked – looked –

' . . . cleaned the place up, anyway,' said Vincent, breathing hard. The work had been demanding.

'What about me?' screamed Lawlor.

'What about you?'

'My place – it cost me to install all this – '

135

'The Ring will see to all that. That is why we permit the Ring. Go see them, Lawlor.'

Dirk Havergen's body lay on a pallet. The rictus of his shocked mouth had set into a feline foolish grin.

'We'll send down for the body later.' Vincent finished cracking out his orders as he strode for the door. 'If you value your hide, Lawlor, you'll wish we find out who did it – for you look to be number one suspect.'

'No! But I didn't – not me – ' Lawlor had been reduced to a failed and flaccid pile of fluff, chance-blown, forgettable.

'Why on this Earth he took his badges off – well – the idiot deserved to die, I suppose, if he did that.'

'Undoubtedly,' said Zack Conrad smoothly.

Vincent glanced at the young man sharply. In his dark face there lay more than a suggestion of ruthless power-craving, a syndrome that had destroyed more men before Adolf Sturm, and would still do so, no matter that any man's prime concern was with his trips.

'I knew there would be nothing here,' Vincent growled, dismissing that flashing image of Conrad. 'I need to carry out a few tests and then Sturm can hear from me. He must be very annoyed you were cut off.'

Conrad braced himself. 'I'll expect you to explain that, Vincent. I'm not taking the can back for your high-handed – '

'Enough!' Vincent glared him down. 'Popinjay! Get out to the flier!' His lush square beard bristled up like a forest of pikes. 'I'm taking the flier – you can leave your ridiculous electric car for the Assessors.'

Storming through the protests of the Assessors, summoned when Havergen's body had been discovered, Vincent led Conrad out like a battleship towing a tanker. He scattered the Assessors before him.

In the tension of the moment Conrad felt happy to fall in behind. He, too, had been having ideas since the city-catastrophe broke.

Over the ziggurat steps of the old city, passing above the monolithic blocks of colossal architecture with their blue and orange glazed bricks, their glass and plastic whirling lines, their solidity of granite and marble and concrete, the flier carried them. Looking down, Vincent said: 'Strange what architectronic fancies can breed from angles of lines and tangents. These systems must now relate to living architecture as the dinosaur to the primates.'

Conrad did not reply. He did not often experience flight over the city.

Vincent misunderstood that silence. 'You don't know what I'm talking about, do you Zack?'

'Huh – oh, sure – just that – '

'I wonder.' Vincent mused heavily. Then, slowly, he said: 'When the Industrial Revolution began, the need for semi-skilled workers leaped prodigiously. To operate the new machines successfully and make a profit for the masters the working classes had to have some degree of education. Oh – not a proper education, that one might achieve at a University. But the three famous old whores, the Three AAHs – aah – how they brought on the birchings. But the kids must learn enough to run a mill, to draught plans, to teach – or half-teach – other kids for the insatiable maws of industry. Elementary education for all so that there should be a great mass of semi-literate workers to perform the work uneducated farm yokels could never master.'

'Yes. I know – some of that education rebounded – a little demanded a taste for more – '

'Sure. So sops were brought in. Everyone's standard of living rose a little, enough to bribe them with TV and fish and chips and bingo and a spurious sense of belonging to the tide of history. The age of Material Plenty had a fine festering base to build upon.'

'Well – they had a little more than that,' said Conrad. 'I mean – motor boats and yachts, fishing and shooting in Alaska, skin-diving in the Bahamas, private flying if you dodged the jets fast enough – '

'All very clever ways of structuring time, boy! That was a transition period, a time out of joint, when the workers thought they were as good as us. That was a tiny ugly period between proper times, when workers are pushed face down in the muck – where they belong.'

'I agree to that. And when full automation came in the masses of half-educated workers were no longer required.' Conrad chuckled. 'At least – '

Vincent chuckled, too. Precisely. We don't want workers to work! We want workers for their Joy Juice!'

Immediately both men felt dry, the craving for Joy Juice ripe and rank within them, goose-pimpling their skin and thickening their tongues. 'I need a shot!' said Conrad, licking his lips.

'Wait until we get back. That'll be my first concern; before even seeing Sturm.' Vincent would enjoy his life spirit from his own accumulators, blue jars with the silver patina upon them, what Conrad did was up to Conrad.

Rousing himself as the flier circled to pass the arrogant and half-ruined mass of Peace Tower, tall among a city of tall structures, once peopled by cunningly insane fantoccini, Vincent carried on his thread of thought in this conversation that laid a foundation for what he would say to Sturm. Sturm maintained strict standards for his own Insurance Company. More than once Vincent had considered the temptation to leave him for someone, else – Snortsen, Karen Oldenshaw, Nadler. But the effort was too much. Although – although if what this youngster Zack Conrad told him was thought out, two members of Sturm's Insurance Company had been killed and vengeance still bayed unappeased. Not comforting reflections, Vincent realised, and yet practical in the modern nasty world-decline of standards – Sturm's as well as anyone else's. If you couldn't trust your own Insurance Company to kill your murderer – who could you trust?

His delight in sampling the strange byways of the old city and savouring their hallucinatory offerings in tripjoints here and there would have to be scrutinised. He had not felt great fear that Lawlor or one of his clients would kill him. They might wish to. But in the confines of the tripjoint the Assessors, blasting on high-speed fliers on the call of his badge, would have arrested the right man in no time at all. Air prints, when the very air itself was sampled and forced to yield up the identities of those present on the scene of the killing, would have fingered the killer unerringly.

But now?

Change and decay all about him festered and laughed.

'Dammit all to hell!' Vincent burst out abruptly, jerking Conrad back in the seat, eyes wide. 'You can't even find a little peace and quiet in a hallucic any more!'

'You can say that again,' said Conrad, morosely.

'Yes, well. I have a shrewd idea why that is; but as for Sturm; he has a lot to answer for! Wake up, boy!'

Conrad wanted to say: 'Ah, get lost!' but, Vincent being Vincent, he refrained. A man's moods shot up and down like a hot geyser when he couldn't get a shot of the right stuff, when he waited overlong for his Joy Juice. One minute he felt frayed and limp; the next morose and suicidal; the next frenetically energetic and working hard for the next shot.

They swooped around a decaying block of apartment houses perched above a power station and someone from a shattered window shot at them. The bullets sang nowhere near the flier; the evil winking dot of orange flame from the window their only clue.

Conrad jerked his own gun out.

Vincent laughed coarsely, and said: 'Forget him, Zack! The city's not itself today. I'm the man who knows the answers and can put them to work for us. So leave that disgruntled worker to the gangs.'

'They should have killed off all the workers a long time ago,' said Conrad, feeling light-headed. 'Joy Juice – I don't know – '

'You want a long life, don't you, boy? Well, then! We may not want workers; but we have to have them fawning and cringing on us, we have to be responsible for their petty little lives. Why – the breeding problem is getting troublesome; damn fool workers spend all their spare time in hallucics instead of in bed procreating.'

'But that's an old problem, surely – '

'Yes. There was a big power failure back in the mid-twentieth century – I know that time – and people couldn't go out easily, no elevators, no television, no radio, no lights. So they couldn't follow their normal pattern of behaviour. Nine months later the birthrate leaped spectacularly. Fact.'

'I see the connection. But we must *make* the workers breed!'

'We do. I have my system. Just so long as we produce enough workers – from worker stock – I don't want a child of mine running around with a worker brand on him – we'll be all right, Jack.'

With the general oppression of fear over hallucinations blanketing the city, Conrad felt Vincent must be confident of his ability to solve the problem – otherwise, Conrad shivered, otherwise the big bearded man was hypnomanic.

139

Sturm stood in a high place, railed with gilded scrollwork, shielded by green and amber shadows, looking down into the lighted hall below. Here waited supplicants, friends with something on their mind, purveyors of fresh treasures from the looted galleries of the world, and, in the present instance, workers waiting to be drained. They did not know, very naturally and properly, that they were to be drained. But the Uppers would have the Joy Juice out of them before nightfall.

Archbold swallowed. 'Hanson marched 'em hard. They're pretty well done in.' His gaunt face harshened against the shadows. 'But I'm sure we'll find they have plenty of effluvia to spare.'

'You'd kill them all then, Archbold?'

'Why not?'

Sturm looked at the chief executive and reflected that it was just as well no one bothered what happened after they died – not any longer, that was – for no sane man would wish to leave an empire he had created in the succeeding hands of John Archbold.

'I'll tell you why. We human beings use up our life spirit the more we live life; asleep we scarcely disturb it, so that when drugged these workers give their vital forces to us without problems. You wish to remove enough from these tired workers to satisfy you and if in the process you kill them you do not worry – '

'No. Of course not. They're workers!'

'And we need workers to provide Joy Juice and the workers grow less every year for they do not breed easily. If you could guarantee me that all those women down there would be made pregnant by you, then, after the births, you could kill them.'

Archbold grimaced. 'No child of mine – ' he began truculently.

'Precisely. We Uppers have no hold on life so we prate of our children, our potential children. What difference does it make to you what happens to a woman and her brat?'

'I wish to control my children until they are old enough to go on the main line themselves, or to take their own Joy Juice shots – '

'The old fear, John, the old fear. No wonder parents used to sacrifice their children to a Phoenician god; no wonder the old

140

Christians put a stop to it, that was the sort of thing Christians used to do, trying to improve human nature and make men and women more decent – poor devils. The ancient fear of new life, shooting up and displacing the old, the new young bull challenging the king, the king to die every winter and be born again – we understand why you don't want your children running around without your knowledge, John.'

'Well? And –'

Sturm looked down more closely.

'We'll take effluvia this night, well enough – the real raw alive stuff, direct from them to us, without the tedious process of running it through the phone lines and bottling it in blue jar accumulators. . . . But we'll do it so we keep them alive. We *need* the workers now, John. . . .'

'Your orders –'

'Yes. We need them; but we need them cowed. If they resist – then they must be slaughtered like streptococci!'

Archbold gripped his fists together, then, to change the direction of the dialogue he nodded down to the hall where the workers sat about, dry and thirsty after their march, dazed and apathetic. 'There she is.'

Sturm looked. He felt a dry rustling excitement begin in his stomach and flood out through his body like sheet lightning suffusing a midnight sky. He swallowed. He stared again at the girl and then, producing the pocket telescope he always carried with him to view the treasures of his room, he spied on her through the lens.

'You won't be draining her!' he told Archbold curtly.

'I thought not.' Archbold spoke with elaborate evenness, without inflection.

'Have her sent to the Chinese room.'

'Yes. Do you want one of the women to look out for her, or shall I process her through the harem – ?'

Sturm turned his eye away from the girl, lowering the telescope, delicately pressing it shut. 'If ever you flattered yourself, John, that you understand me – forget any thought of self-praise.' Sturm pushed past, leaving the glassed gallery with its emerald and umber shadows. 'Send her just as she is, dirty, bedraggled, sweat stained. There is, John, rather a fine bath in the Chinese room.'

'Yes, Sturm,' said John Archbold, his cindery face scrubbed as though by pumice.

The soles of his feet burned.

The stitch in his side burned.

His eyes burned.

But he knew without a single doubt that this was the reality of the outer world. At his side Minch moaned softly, and rolled over, her smock dragging against her smooth, rounded, funny leg. All about them in this lofty shadow-shrouded hall with the lights burning down concentratedly on them, the other workers huddled, dazed and woebegone and frightened. They all spoke in whispers.

'Shut up crying, Minch,' Sheldon said, crossly.

'But I'm frightened – and I need a fix.'

'So do we all. I'm shivering inside like wet cement.'

'You said you had a needle – and some stuff ...'

'Yeah, well – we might be moved in a minute, and – '

'You're going to keep it all for yourself, that's what you're going to do!'

Sheldon looked at her, and ...

... Drowning, drifting, choking, sea urges spuming stupefyingly over them, her white gown drifting in sea spray, her body pressed close – *close*! – her left leg dragging, smooth and rounded, his own body enwrapped with hers. ...

They both floundered on the floor, shaking, the nudism a mystic bond and partitioner, soul-shaking.

'All right!' Sheldon snapped, hard and hating. 'So I'm keeping the stuff for myself. What are you going to do about it, Minch, away?'

She stared back at him with her massy hair falling forward, her arms pressed down with her palms flat against the floor, her eyes downcast, beaten and soft and lonely.

'I – ' she said, in a gush of abnegation. 'I can't do anything, can I, Sheldon?'

'Just remember that – '

He did not finish. Four Uppers, the guns in their hands glittering under the lights focussed here, walked in step across the floor, kicking out of the way workers who did not move fast enough. Sheldon scrabbled out of their way. Minch, struggling

142

up, falling forward, gasped as her leg dragged.

One Upper grasped her about the shoulders, another seized her legs, clumsily bundling them together. She was hoisted like a sack in a forklift. The four Uppers, stiff and grim without feeling, marched away, taking Minch with them.

Sheldon stared after them, feeling confused, thoughts and ideas chasing themselves like lightning flashes in his brain. He shook his head. 'Well,' he said. 'I won't have to share the stuff now.'

12

The meeting between Adolf Eric Sturm and Arthur Vincent Cheesman took place on a high-flying platform within the treasure-choked hangar of Sturm's room.

Sturm had climbed there, telescope under arm, to meditate in peace on his forthcoming conquest. He would never seek to rush so important a physical activity. Absolution had brought him far in this muddled modern world and his ruthlessness demanded every now and then the recuperation afforded only by withdrawal into a private place.

He knew himself to be an isolated specimen of humanity. Even Vincent, for all his strengths, had no interest in the world of outer reality. Sturm's interest, even when tuned to its highest pitch, could only be fragmentary. As now, when he languidly surveyed the gathered outpourings of the human spirit, or when he went to his harem, or even – and here the flame of involvement flickered more fiercely – when he took a young and crippled girl. These more concrete shadows against the deeper shadows of life held a tiny power to halt Sturm and to draw him momentarily back from the vital and important issues of the inner self, of the dreaming inscapes of his mind.

He knew that he would see this whole room, this whole enormous collection of art and beauty, he would see the harem and the crippled girls – all of them, vanished, gone in a puff of smoke, denied completely if they stood between him and the enjoyment of his drugged hallucinations.

He would see Vincent shot and dragged into the gutter to lie rotting there if he could not solve the terrible question of the hour. If the hallucinations could no longer be enjoyed, Sturm couldn't care less about the collapse of the world, the chaos as workers and Uppers ran wild. He saw with frightful clarity that he – he, Sturm! – would no longer be able to enjoy those precious hours wandering the channels and labyrinths of his own mind.

Vincent walked slowly towards him along the narrow railed platform. Blued by distance the walkways and alleyways between beauty opened before them. The air hung in limpid clarity, perfumed, deodorised, conditioned, around them. Below them rank on rank of pictures, paintings, books, statuary and sculpture descended a staircase of culture to the floor. In a corner of the platform a great coptic jar, all whirling lines and fluid forms, glazed, brilliant, enigmatic, sprouted a flowing droop of giant ferns, soft and cool and green with the green of primeval swamps. Beneath their natural shade within the artificial environment a white iron seat squatted on lion-claws. Plump foam cushions, velvet-covered, buttoned, braided, smothered the seat in luxury.

Sturm sat down, leaned back, tilted his square bristly head.

Vincent halted five feet off, his massive beard out-thrust, his piercing eyes piercing now into reflections of themselves. Here were met two men, two peers, two masters.

Negligently, Sturm indicated the seat.

Vincent leaned against the gilt and scrolled railing, high above the cultured-staircase, his face unreadable and contained. He knew Sturm of old. He understood what twisted forces drove the squat over-muscled man on.

'Well, Vincent,' Sturm burst out, at last. 'Well?'

Leaning against the railing, one hand thrust deeply into his pocket, Vincent looked away from Sturm, out over that domed vastness. He saw with reminiscent pleasure many objects of eternal beauty he had met within the confines of his own brain.

Sturm blazed like a pugnacious firecracker among dinner guests. 'Come on, Vincent! You must know the answer! What's been happening? Why are our drugs failing us?'

'When did you last have a – pleasant – hallucic, Adolf?'

'When? Oh – I don't know! Let me see – Yes, it must be at least a week, probably more.' He looked up defensively. 'Sometimes only the tail end goes sour. Nothing really serious perturbed me – we all know from time to time we have a black hallucic and know why – '

'We used to say that a bad hallucination visited us as a

spice, in order to make us the more appreciate the normal experience.' Vincent's chuckle sounded like a death wind beneath a cracked tomb stone.

'So? Everybody's been suffering the same things, even the workers. Now – now it's burst. I can't go on like this, Vincent.'

'Neither can I. If you'd seen what I've seen – myself, condemning myself. I saw people I've met before in hallucinations, and this time they cheapened me, made me feel small, made me see things I didn't want to see. And every one was myself.'

'Of course.' Sturm stood up, unable to sit down while Vincent leaned against the railing. 'Everyone we meet in hallucinations is ourselves. We're not peddling dreams – dreams are kiddies' palliatives.' He thumped a hand into his palm, a flat smack. 'I commanded a legion to advance and rout the elephants – and they turned on me – me! – and I had to run for it with pila flying past my ears. It aged me.'

'Joy Juice will take care of that,' Vincent said curtly.

'And when the target line of battlecruisers began firing back and hitting with fifteen inchers – you know, Vincent, it isn't pleasant to be straddled and hit and chucked into the drink with fifty thousand tons turning over in the water and dragging you down with it – '

'My inclinations haven't tended in those – ah – physical directions, Adolf. My cases were more needling, more – ah – subtle. A good symbolist is needed to penetrate to the whole meanings of what I went through. But I appreciate enough.' He pushed himself up and said: 'By the way, I know what's causing all the trouble.'

'Well, for God's sake, man! Tell me!'

'I wish I could place that damned leopard woman in the right perspective, though,' Vincent said ruminatively.

'I have leopard woman, too,' Sturm said impatiently. He moved towards Vincent. 'But tell me what the trouble is!'

'You do? That's interesting. You see, if she is a symbol for – '

'I shoot mine. Now – '

'I used to, Adolf. But this time around I could never, somehow, lay my hands on a gun. A used bus ticket, not a gun. Damned odd – and frightening.'

'If you don't tell me what the trouble is – '

'Yes, yes.' Vincent saw his cat and mouse with Sturm must

be terminated. As a new gambit in the game the young Uppers played he felt it would prove the winner – if they survived it. 'It is all your own fault.'

Sturm's face suffused with blood. His bristles appeared to move, a silly thought but one which the lighting and the constriction of the skin on his face made very terribly a thing in which one would believe. 'My fault?' he said softly, stalkingly.

'Yours, and everyone else's.' Vincent hurried the next words. 'You know about sensitization?'

'Yes, of course. Well, that is – '

'So I'll tell you.'

Sturm remained silent; but his head like the square horrible mask on an Egyptian sarcophagus, thrust forward with a violent tension. 'So tell me.'

'When antibotics first came on to the market medical people used them like crazy and the microbes adapted in double-quick time. Living organisms, if not killed off stone-dead first time around, have a habit of adapting to hostile environments. Pretty soon the governments of those days had to clamp down, allow the use of broad-spectrum and synthesised antibiotics only in the most desperate of needs.'

'I see your drift. But they were bugs – '

'The human body, to coin a phrase, is built up of specialised bugs.'

'Ah – ye-es.'

'A person who couldn't take an antibiotic was called a sensitive. A nice little euphemism. But it adds up to what has happened to us. Gradually the human body has built up not an immunity to drugs – that won't come, or hasn't yet – but a capacity to deal semi-effectually with the sophisticated drugs we use. You can still get a crude warm glow from hashish, or opium, or one of the other primitive drugs. But they cannot give you the level of intensification of experience in hallucination our modern drugs can give – '

'So our own body cells are fighting the drugs – '

Vincent sighed. 'I prognosticated you would say that. No – not that, well, not exactly. That's a crude infantile way of expressing what is, essentially, a most complex series of functions. The body is, in its own way, striking back at the drug, trying to adapt, to find a way to do what all life must do, that is, expand. The body structure is sending up all sorts of alarm

147

signals to the brain; and the brain can only react by triggering alarm on a mental level. Our chemotherapeutic systems, our health disciplines, our gymnasium workouts, ensure that purely physical breakdown won't trouble us.'

A small screen in the corner, to one side of the drooping ferns, lit up and Archbold said: 'She's in the Chinese room, Sturm. All ready.'

'Right, John,' Sturm said bleakly, not taking his eyes off Vincent. 'I'll be down presently.' The screen died.

Vincent didn't bother to enquire. He knew about Sturm and his little ways with little littles.

'So our bodies have at last caught up with us – '

'With the abuse we have been subjecting them to for a good long time.' Vincent put both hands on the gilded railing, looking out over the fantastic jumble of precious works of art. 'We've taken, Sturm. Taken all along the line. Not just humanity as a whole; but us, as the Uppers, a small clique of fortunate men and women. We've taken what life can give, what the workers give us, what the treasure vaults of past ages can give – and we've taken what our own bodies can give us. Now one of the victims is protesting. Our bodies have decided that they will register a protest. So we have poison in our hallucinations.'

'As the others,' Sturm said off-handedly, thinking along the most important line, 'the treasures are here, or some of them – what's scattered about over the rest of the world doesn't interest me – and we will continue to take what life can give us.'

'Life.' Vincent turned and stared sombrely at Sturm. 'I wonder if any of us any longer knows what life is all about.'

'Rubbish. Now we'll have to set up a programme – '

'Rubbish, Adolf? I don't know. Our whole story is like a stained glass window, fantasy the glass, and reality the lead framing.'

Sturm sneered. 'That's a very pretty illumination, Vincent. And if you look at the relative beauty and excitement of the lead and the glass in a stained glass window you'll see the relative values; the glass, our hallucinations, is by far the more valuable.'

'I cannot argue with that.' Vincent's forehead creased.

'But I think that it is the lead framing that holds the picture together.'

Sturm looked at him narrowly. 'What are you going to do about it, Vincent? We must programme – '

'Oh, I'm sure we'll find a way around it. The computer will be invaluable. Machines once more galloping to the rescue of homo sapiens.'

'You sound – empty, Vincent. Dry?'

'You know damn well we're all dry.'

'Too true. You never realise – realise fully, I mean, – how much the inner landscapes of the mind mean until you are deprived of them.' He licked his lips again. 'And that Karen Oldenshaw started me off on that stupid bit about inner landscapes. I told her they were inscapes – '

Vincent shook his head. He had found a Modigliani and was tracing the curve of the neck and marvelling at the impish sauce of this perfect exuberance. 'I've told her that she's wrong; but she insists. Whoever first thought of the words inner landscapes to define the inner life of the mind, the hallucinated super ego, the id at large, knew little about the abstract symbolism of life.'

'We'll put everyone on the computer programming – '

'The land surface is where we know ourselves, where we feel sure, in command; this is our waking self. But the deeper depths of our psyche which we plumb when we are drugged and in which we experience the hallucinatory schizophrenia of dreams so wild and full of terrors as the sea is full of strangeness, this is our unconscious. We do not explore inner landscapes; but inner seascapes. We came from the sea and we are tied by sleep symbolically to the sea. All man's irrational impulses and the submerged drives that propel him it seems helplessly about the landscapes of reality surge with primitive power in the oceans of his mind.'

'Inner seascapes. Well, yes. Of course. But what – ?'

'I'll get some of our young men on the computer right away. As for the Moral Aid people; they must be smashed. The free and open use of hallucinofabs must be made universal until we have solved this drug problem.'

Sturm smiled wickedly. 'You never use a lucimech yourself, Vincent.'

'No. I prefer more control. The workers can't control their

hallucinations and so they don't expect too much; I not only control mine, I programme lucimechs; but programming a lucimech for a dumb worker is different from subjecting yourself to its whims.'

Sturm, whose craggy strength had at one time appeared ready to splinter, now strode about with renewed zest. In a world of dissolving shadows he at least would attend the last random disintegration with a drugged vivacity.

'The stupid workers revolt will collapse the moment we stop the drugs and turn off the lucimech power. Now that we know the answer – at least, that you are working on it, Vincent – we must think about this damn worker procreation problem.'

'We're Uppers, Adolf. What we say goes.'

'I know. Of course. So?'

'So I can guarantee you overcoming two problems with one sleight-of-hand.'

'This sounds interesting – '

'It is. Pick me out a young strong worker and a young pretty girl. You have some hostages or something below, I believe.'

'Yes.' Sturm shot a nasty look at Vincent. The two men were too valuable to each other now for any violence to flare between them, but . . .

. . . all around ice, snow shrieking past them, black wind, numbing cold that rang great icicle gongs in their heads; Sturm and Vincent holding each the arm of a fur coat, their naked bodies blue and goosepimpled and swiftly sliding into frozen immobility and death, and tugging, tugging, tugging for the fur coat. . . .

Their faces pale and sweat-streaked, gasping, both men staggered back a pace or two on the railed platform in the room of treasure.

'You bastard!' grated Sturm, gripping the rail.

'You – get off me!' snarled Vincent. The feel of the ice and snow and the flaying lash of the wind sickened him, frightened him.

'No one takes a nudism off me without – '

'Nor me, Adolf. I've experienced newdisms that were marvellous, wonderful – I remember Patsy – but this – this was obscene!'

'Not obscene, Vincent. Just true. But, so help me, if you try anything at all, any single little trick at all – '

'Save your threats, Sturm. We need each other for the moment. If I have to kill you after that, I will, don't fret.'

Breathing hard, clashing his muscles together, Sturm said: 'Wait and see. Now let me see what you have planned with these two workers.'

The great goldfish bowl of the city tightened in glassy spirals around the lives swarming dolorously within.

Sheldon fingered his badge. Much good it would do him now when all his clique were either gathered in here or powerless to help him no matter what happened. He knew well enough the worker badges were mere imitations of the Uppers' badges and he knew, too, from the fierce speed with which Uppers arrived on the scene of trouble that they had been summoned by some cybernetic system or other; but these thoughts meant nothing beside the feel of togetherness the spurious badges engendered. He liked to think, did Sheldon, liked to allow his mind to play around with tortous ideas and concepts. He would have made a good Upper, he had thought, betraying his class with careless longing.

'You! Here!'

The Upper, clad all in black tights, a helmet globular and somehow tadpolish on his head, beckoned. The truncheon with which he beckoned spoke most eloquently.

Sheldon scrambled awkwardly to his feet and shambled between two Uppers into a small room. Here – over-riding his protests and taking great delight in their handling – the Uppers removed his clothes and his possessions. He watched them take his needle. They threw the packet of drugs down on a table without a second look. They were not too cruel with him; merely indifferent.

He wondered, numbly, if they knew he had killed one of their people. He hoped they didn't know. But he hoped with more aliveness that they would give him back his needle and his stuff.

The cold shaking quagmire of need for a fix groped up his body, gripping his throat, gagging him. Vague remembrances of angry colours, flamingly cruel colours, tantalised him with the freshest wells of pure experience waiting for him within the hollow needle tip.

Sweat hung thick and reeking on his forehead. Around him

he could see the Uppers and see their similar need and see nothing in it touching his own condition. He could sense everything of himself and nothing of them. The memory of Minch meant only one less greedy grasp on his needle and store of drugs.

If they didn't give him the stuff soon . . .

'Take him through there.' The Upper who spoke, wearing dark blue slacks and shirt, wore like them all the badge of covetous need. Slouching where he was directed, Sheldon saw the Upper and a shutter clicked open in his mind. Yes. This man had been striding up to shoot him when he'd thrown the knife to settle the hash of that prowling Upper that night he'd met Minch beneath the broken flyover. . . .

The dark memory of that warmed Sheldon, warmed him more as he recalled what he had done in hallucination with his knife to the knife-fighter; this aloof Upper had not recognised him, for sure.

They went through into a small square green-plastered room with a plastic table and no chairs. Standing in one corner were two men. Sheldon glanced indifferently at them. He saw they were Uppers, he saw the square mass of beard of the one and the short squat squareness of the other; but they meant nothing to him. On the table, alone and in glorious isolation, lay a needle and the familiar white packet of Central Welfare packaged drugs.

The muscle-bound one said: 'Will this one do, Vincent?'

The man with the beard said: 'Excellently. He looks strong enough. I deplore the breakdown of the old Eugenics Board. Now that we are forced to breed without strict controls all manner of incompatibles are allowed to mate. Homo sapiens should always have the fullest Eugenic testing before reproduction is allowed.' He frowned absently at Sheldon. 'Bring him over here, Zack.'

The young Upper prodded Sheldon, who slommicked across.

He had no real idea what they were talking about. All he could see, feel, sense, hear and desire lay on the table.

'I take it, Sturm,' said the bearded man, 'you will wish to witness the act yourself?'

'Of course. It will act as a pleasant – ah – stimulator for – ah – later.'

'Quite.'

'When,' spoke up Sheldon. 'When do I get to take a trip?'

'All in good time, worker, all in good time. Now that you're passed you must come through here – ' Sheldon felt a vague overpowering sense of forces with which he could come to no understanding moving in ways mysterious beyond belief. Cowed, his one spurt of defiance spent, he went through into the room beyond. His relief when the Upper picked up the needle and the packet of drugs drained him.

The granite faces around him seemed to seep a poison into the air so that he longed for the smoother marble walls of his familiar pad,

'There's a couch.'

Sheldon took a single uninterested glance at the room; its yellow walls, windowless and low, the door at the far end, the rugs patterning in brown and gold over the tiled floor; he let himself down on the couch and took the needle and drugs into his own hands.

The Uppers, after a final few words, left and the door shut.

'He's a self-centred one,' said Conrad, closing the door.

'Maybe not, Zack.' Vincent had not dabbled in psycho-probing for some time and he did not intend to begin again now. 'But he will do for this experiment. We'd better go up.'

The three men stepped into the lift and were wafted to the mezzanine above the rooms forming this small annexe to Sturm's broader complex of rooms and chambers. Sturm tumbled the switch that polarised the floor and lower wall of this room so that they could sit back comfortably in overstuffed chairs and look down directly at the play beneath.

'This had better work, Vincent,' growled Sturm. 'I don't intend to waste my time sitting here for nothing.'

'I think you will find it quite extraordinarily successful. We are in reality now. I have furnished that worker with a harm-less drug that will for a brief moment convince his body tissues they have been fed the right stuff. His mind – '

'You might fool the body – but the mind?'

'The placebo effect is on our side. He is taking a drug; there-fore anything that happens afterwards is hallucination. *Quod erat demonstrandum.* Or something.' Vincent, like them all, felt the pangs of dry need spiking into his guts.

'*Faciendum,*' growled Sturm, impatiently.

'I know, I know,' snapped Vincent. 'I just hope the girl

153

feels like it at the right time. We fed her a well-chosen aphrodisiac; but the time-lag can alter catastrophically with bodily changes – '

'I know, also,' Sturm said cuttingly. 'If it was as easy as feeding them aphrodisiacs and letting them loose there would be no problem, would there?'

Conrad moved in his chair. 'He's just hit the pike,' he said, enviously. 'He's taking the mainline – '

'For gosh-sakes!' exploded Vincent. 'That's a placebo job on down there, Zack. You're not jealous? Haw, haw!' he finished crudely.

Sturm shifted, like Conrad, impatient. 'We're all falling to pieces,' he said in his gravel voice. 'Hell – why don't we all cut our throats and have done with it?'

'You cut your throat any damn time you like, Sturm.' Vincent fiddled out a cigarette case and handed around the reefers, casually. 'Try a candy bar while we wait.'

'Keep that kid stuff,' Sturm said heavily. He produced his own case. 'I'll fire up the ack-ack gun. He'd better be good,' he said, darkly. 'He better be good.'

Everyone else in the city could feel the hunger for a fix devouring their insides, burning their desires into a pyre of immolation – Sheldon was not alone in venturing once more upon those hostile oceans of the mind to assuage a world nausea.

The memory of immediate experience faded before the lowering weight of habit and need. In a zeitegeist firmly centred around drugs and lucimechs whose very existence created their own need the flavour of life soured reluctantly. Sheldon was no Upper. But he could understand that any breakdown of the pattern of reality and hallucination would mean the end of civilisation as he knew it.

A weltanschauung of the most simple surface kind might satisfy Sheldon and his fellow workers. He didn't care what would satisfy the Uppers.

A single spark of light lived at the tip of the needle.

He lay back on the couch after he had quenched that spark in his veins.

Contact.

The room remained where it was. The yellow walls remained

yellow; the rugs remained brown and gold. The ceiling stayed on the room. Beneath his hands, trembling and yet eager for touch stimuli, the couch remained a couch. He closed his eyes, ecstasy in anticipation fibrillating his lashes against his cheeks whose warmth faded and coarsened like a danger signal abandoned by the rusty speedways.

He heard the faintest hum from oiled machinery. He opened his eyes. Colours dripped down the walls, writhing like electric snakes, flouerescing and coruscating, flaring across the walls like a sunset and sunrise battling for supremacy on a forgotten planet. He watched, mildly interested, waiting for the big time.

Everybody now and then, he knew, experienced colours during a trip; he possessed a natural arrogance of knowledge that only he experienced colours of intensity and vision of true value. His colours were better than anyone else's.

Discomfiting and vague ideas of dissatisfaction with his colours whirling about him and were lost like gossamer veils as the far door opened and a girl glided through. Sheldon sat up on the couch, slowly, cautiously, wondering when the floor might open, wondering if the girl would fleet past him with a dying lingering look. The girl walked across the floor towards him. She did not limp.

For some reason that, whilst annoying him also, had power, now, to disturb him, the idea of this girl walking on two strong and perfect legs upset him. She should walk with her left knee tucked in behind the right.

He saw that she wore gossamer veils, a multitude of jewellery, a glowing smile and a hairdo that might once have graced the head of a courtesan. Her smile engulfed him. Her eyes had been kohled into purple-blue invitations. Her teeth shone. She breathed quickly and shallowly, fluttering her draperies, and the tip of her tongue showed cherry red.

Sheldon quite liked her.

She reminded him of Deedee.

He stood up, in his own hallucination not troubled at all that he stood naked, rather, joying in his freedom; in the freedom of such different nuances from the sterile freedom of the gym.

She smiled.

'Do you like me, Sheldon?'

155

'Oh, yes – of course. You remind me of Deedee.'

'Silly boy. I am Deedee.'

He had never met Deedee before in a hallucic. It might be fun. He remembered picking up her button, covering her breast, pulling down her smock. She looked different now. A jib-job-jab of the old needle could brighten anything up. He perked up. She went on smiling at him.

Over in the corner of the room an area suddenly lit up with white light, very much like an ancient cinema screen, and vaguely out-of-focus events took place there as music strained through the odorous scents dropping from the ceiling.

Sheldon caught hold of Deedee's arm. It felt solid and comfortingly real. With the physical contact, flesh against flesh, his fear that she would dissolve and vanish like a phantom dissipated. He could possess her at his leisure without fear, now, that she would change into a scavenging black beetle.

The strangeness of his illusion amused rather than bothered him. Spice, said the Uppers, was the change of life. They went on and on and seemed to age rarely. As he drew Deedee down on to the couch and stripped off her gossamer he even had time to think for a fleeting and amazed moment of Minch. Well – you never knew – he might encounter her after he'd toyed long enough with Deedee. She was all over him now, biting and gnawing and pulling – the idea of Minch faded a little more. The lack of clarity about this hallucination began to be rectified.

Events sharpened.

. . . and he looked out at himself through Deedee's eyes, startled and white and close, straining, panting, gripping as this body that was his gripped and gripped himself, one entity, one body, one flesh. . . .

The nudism died.

He held Deedee's body in his arms, cradled close. He looked down on her face, half-smiling, lips barely touching so that the skin clung damply, her eyes closed so that their lids formed those subtle mounds of flesh, blue-veined, he looked down on her and wondered that he could experience so vivid a nudism within a hallucination. But he did not wonder long. Deedee was very demanding.

He missed the hallucinatory clarity of his colours; but with Deedee he found something he had been missing on most of his recent trips. He found, too, a satiety that had eluded him for too long. No memories of that monstrous molochian island-mouth, that coral wind-swept path, those skull-littered deserts ruined his trip this time around.

Really, Sheldon felt he had a first class trip, when he considered. . . .

'There you are. I told you so.' Vincent pulled his beard with jovial satisfaction. He felt a personal sense of triumph. 'Clean as a whistle. He thought like she did the whole thing was a hallucinatory experience. And, if they've clicked we've given them a little stake in the future, and ensured another little worker for our own purposes.'

On the couch below them the nude bodies with the anaesthetic darts still sticking in their flesh were being removed by emotionless Upper nursemaids brought down from the nursery on Sturm's orders. They handled Sheldon and Deedee with an unconcern that reflected their own inner absorption with their own problems, and in that they merely shared the world neurosis.

'You could have fooled me,' Conrad said, breathily.

'A most illuminating experience.' Sturm's eyes showed a bright and febrile glitter from the lights in the room. 'Most salutary. I must congratulate you, Vincent, on achieving the seemingly impossible. Why' – he spoke with vivacity, now, standing up and striding stockily about – 'Why, this opens up an entirely new field! Those poor fools actually believed they were experiencing a hallucination, they thought they were taking a trip and indulging in a dream love affair, afloat on the oceans of their minds – '

'Yes – ' Vincent ran his tongue around his teeth. 'If only it was as easy to fool us – '

'Rubbish, man! Don't you see it yet?' Sturm rounded on him, bubbling with excitement. 'I'll have a similar charade arranged – and I'll withdraw the Joy effluvia from the next pair of them right in the middle of – '

'But,' broke in Vincent, his feeling of annoyance directed at a mistaken notion of his work, 'but we need workers still. That way you'd probably kill both of them.'

'What a way to die,' said Conrad, the jealousy of Sturm's casual acceptance of all-power rankling.

'So perhaps they might.' Sturm clearly now saw the way ahead. He felt magnified, possessed, elated. 'I thought a sewn-up saga offered the most for the least – we just stick them in the hammocks, feed them intravenously, siphon off their waste products, and feed them with an intravenous drug-drip. They exist in their happy hunting ground of the mind and we extract a continuous supply of Joy Juice. But this – !'

'The experiment was not conducted for those purposes, Adolf!' Vincent began to walk back to the stair and the elevator. 'I couldn't care less what you do, you know that. But we must ensure worker continuity.'

'But you'll do that, Vincent.' Sturm brushed aside argument. 'And you will attend to this nonsense about our bodies coping with the drugs. You will step up production of hallucinofabs. Everything will turn out all right.'

'Of course I can do that. You panicked unnecesssarily, perhaps. Conrad, here, really thought everything was going down the drain when he woke me up.' Vincent laughed softly. 'The 'Orrible Troof,' he said, gently, thinking of the leopard-woman who had broken that last appointment.

'Why the hell do you think we're Uppers at all?' Sturm's belligerence was not assumed. 'Some of you were born Uppers without even knowing the score. We're Uppers because we're better than the workers. We have more brain-power, more intellect and intelligence and imagination. More bone on the hoof. We're more! It's no good whining that you're a worker and an underdog – if you were any good, mac, you'd be an Upper, along with us.'

They all knew he was talking to the miasmic vision of that archetypal worker who lived, loved a little, worked and died in the old city, the city without a single scrap of greenery, not a plant, not a tree, not a blade of grass among all its concrete and glass and plastic.

'Yes,' nodded Conrad. 'The Uppers *are* upper. We *are* better than the workers. If a worker could fight his way up to be an Upper, well – he'd be worthy to be an Upper.'

Vincent wholeheartedly agreed; but he added: 'We act out the dramas of the workers and batten on them; but we are subject to the same forces, we are caught in the same trap. We are as adjusted as are they.'

'I owe to no set of rules,' growled Sturm. His black-browed

glance challenged Vincent. 'I have read of the days when men were ruled by rules, ordinances, guidelines not fashioned by a rational mind. The law of the Uppers is simple, and you all know it by now.'

'We are still alive,' acknowledged Vincent.

'Oh, yes,' breathed Conrad. He did not bother to feel for the third worker knife. He knew it lay there in its sheath, ready and sweet, waiting to find its predestined home in the heart of baboon-face Reven*ooer*.

If they had done nothing else – as they had indeed – Sheldon and Deedee had created a tiny catharsis in the emotions of the three Uppers who had watched them. Sturm, Conrad and Vincent spoke and acted without that jerky itchiness with which they had begun this experiment. They still hated each other, of course; but everyone hated everyone else these days, it was scarcely worthy of comment.

'Well,' Sturm brusqued up, rubbing his hands, bulging his muscles. 'Let's get on with it.'

'I have – ah – work to attend to.' Conrad walked down the last few steps of the exit as Sturm halted Vincent with a word behind him. Conrad moved on out into the city. Now that Vincent was going to fix up the drugs and everyone could go on a decent trip again, things were back to normal. Now he could attend to baboon-face. The man's Company badge was going to avail him nothing. Conrad had it all worked out.

He glanced behind. Sturm stood like a granite outcrop, blocky and hard. A knife would still slide into that body, glide moistly between his ribs; he was no superman.

Walking on into the city, Conrad began to wonder ...

'. . . and the quicker the better, Vincent,' Sturm was saying. 'Everything's going to be all right now. We'll squash the workers flat to show them we are the Uppers. We'll have the drugs altered so our bodies cannot falsify their instructions. We can now ensure continuing growth of the worker force. And we'll up the rate of joy juice extraction.' He bulged there at the top of the steps, confident and proud and monumental. 'Life is going to be all right again, Vincent.'

'Of course it is.' Vincent knew that. 'We'll just carry on. I must confess I wish to try conclusions again with some of the people in my own trip. That wasp-eyed leopard-woman – she intrigues me.'

'Just get us back to the status quo, Vincent.'

'I'll do that.' Vincent began to walk off, following Conrad. 'Everything is going to be just the same as before.'

'Wonderful,' said Sturm.

He walked back into the foyer of his room, picking up his telescope from a sidetable and tucking it under his arm. There would be no time to browse through the round eye over his collection of art now. He felt good. He would enjoy this one. He particularly admired the way her leg still retained its roundness and plumpness and the way it tucked into the back of the other knee. She had a nice little figure, too. And that hair . . . ! Oh, yes, Adolf Eric Sturm really was going to enjoy himself with this one.

Outside under the transparent city roof Vincent thought he saw a scrap of green caught momentarily by a vagrant gleam in the angle of a wall. He didn't bother to go over. Everyone knew the old weed-killer poisons had effectively cleaned up the city. Then he paused. He walked across the concrete road and bent down beside the concrete wall.

In the angle the concrete had cracked, dark winey stains picking out the crumbled edges, a damp odour rising. Looking with disbelief Vincent saw a fingering of limp grass blades, he saw a red-stemmed plant growing, branching and re-branching, climbing up out of that cracked concrete confinement.